PARIS WHEN IT SIZZLES

Julie Kistler

A KISMET® Romance

METEOR PUBLISHING CORPORATION
Bensalem, Pennsylvania

Copyright © 1993 Julie Kistler
Cover Art Copyright © 1993 Paul Bachem

First Printing August 1993.

ISBN: 1-56597-080-2

To Pat Kay, who introduced me to Catherine Carpenter, and to Catherine Carpenter, who couldn't have been lovelier.

JULIE KISTLER

Julie Kistler counts PARIS WHEN IT SIZZLES as her twelfth romance novel. It combines the humor, sparkle, and sense of outrageous fortune Julie enjoys most in life. Julie and her husband visited France on their first wedding anniversary, traveling with backpacks and Eurail passes some twelve years ago. They both have fond memories of champagne and Paris, which is what gave Julie the idea for this book in the first place. Julie and her husband now live outside Champaign, Illinois, with their cat, Thisbe.

ONE

ELVIS'S GHOST APPEARS AT BEDSIDE OF 1,000-POUND
MAN!

That nasty little headline was blinking at the top of
Annie Porter's computer screen. What the heck was
going on?

Annie had just written the Elvis piece and kissed it
good-bye a few hours ago, sending it up to the boss's
office for next week's cover story. Elvis was a sure
thing, guaranteed to sell millions of copies of *Under-cover USA*. But here he was, ghost and all, back again
to haunt her.

"Writing you the first time was bad enough," she
told her headline. "This little revisitation is more than
I can handle."

There was no comment, from Elvis or anyone else.
Absently chewing her lip, Annie called up her message
file for an explanation. Sure enough, there was a terse
note from her boss.

"Our readers prefer their Elvis alive and kicking. No
ghosts. Redo."

"Redo, my foot," Annie muttered. Scowling at the
screen, she backspaced over the headline and typed, I

HATE ELVIS, as if that would furnish inspiration for a new story.

It didn't.

"I hate my job more than I hate Elvis," she said out loud, half expecting lightning bolts to singe her where she sat.

How in the world had it come to this? Who could ever have imagined that Anna Lee Jonesborough Porter, cum laude journalism graduate, would end up as a tabloid hack? Once upon a time, she'd been a *real* reporter, with ethics and integrity. Okay, so she worked for the *Hixville Telegraph-Recorder*, circulation 250 on a good day, and her stories were about bake sales and the junior high marching band. At least she had some connection to reality.

"But no money," she reminded herself sadly. Unfortunately, ethics didn't pay the rent, and *Undercover USA* did.

Boy oh boy, did they pay the rent—fabulously, spectacularly well. And so, at a particularly needy moment in her life, with the bait of a huge salary and an even huger company apartment dangling in front of her dazed eyes, she'd taken it. Hook, line, and sinker.

So here she was, languishing at *Undercover USA*, where "scandal" was their favorite word, and "truth" didn't even make the top fifty.

"Let's see," Annie mused, mentally thumbing through the possibilities for a new Elvis cover story. "Three men and one woman who claim to *be* Elvis, seven who swear they're his children, fifteen who say they slept with him, and one looney-tune who thinks she was his love slave in a previous life on Venus."

It was enough to make a grown woman scream. "I hate my job," she said through gritted teeth. "I swear, with Elvis's ghost as my witness—" she felt like Scarlett O'Hara eating dirt, but she went on anyway "—that I will *leap* at the next chance that comes my way. Whatever it is, no matter how slim the odds, no matter how lousy the pay, I'll take it, and I will get myself out of this place.''

''Hello?'' someone called from the direction of her door, and Annie jumped. Everybody joked that *Undercover*'s offices were bugged, but she'd never taken the rumors seriously. Until now.

Could it be true? Had Big Brother heard all of her disparaging remarks?

She spun around in her chair, expecting the worst. But it was only Tim, the perky young guy who pushed the mail cart.

''Excuse me, Ms. Porter,'' he said quickly, ''but I have a batch of press releases that just came in. Look at this one—fun, huh?''

A fun press release? Annie accepted the stack of papers, glancing down at Tim's ''fun'' flyer, written in swirling pink letters.

ISN'T IT ROMANTIC? A crystal flute of fine champagne . . . a ripe, red raspberry fed to you by your lover . . . Romance at its best . . .

So far Annie was not impressed. ''Too many ellipses,'' she said severely, but she persevered.

Here at Framboise Champagne, where pink champagne is an art form . . .

''Blah, blah, blah,'' she said, skipping ahead. ''Ah yes, this sounds more like it.''

. . . Tell us, in five pages or less, your idea for a lush, romance-filled evening, involving Framboise Champagne.

Who knows? You might just end up one of our four finalists, flown to Paris on the Concorde, treated like royalty, living the romantic life you've always dreamed of. And from among those lucky finalists, we'll choose one truly romantic soul, to travel the world as the new Framboise Champagne Romance Ambassador.

Annie sat up straighter. Unless she missed her guess, they were talking about a job here. Oh, they might be hiding it behind the fancy title of "Romance Ambassador," but Annie knew it for what it was. And what was it? A real, live employment opportunity, that's what, as a public relations person for their champagne. Not only was it a real job, but it was a job that Annie Porter was sure she could handle with one hand tied behind her back.

All of a sudden, this was beginning to sound very interesting.

If your fantasy is the best of the best, and you're chosen as our Romance Ambassador, your days and nights could be filled with exciting travel, to the world's most beautiful cities . . . Vienna, Athens, Rio de Janeiro. . . . You'll be the center of attention at press conferences, television and radio appearances, special parties and receptions in your honor.

Imagine the possibilities. . . .

"Imagine the possibilities," she repeated softly. This was pretty scary. She had no more than asked for a chance when one walked in the door, courtesy of Framboise Champagne.

"Romance Ambassador to the world," she said out loud. "Why not?"

She was a writer, wasn't she? And she'd been creating fantasies for almost two years now. Okay, so her stories were about UFOs and celebrity diets, but surely she could come up with one little romantic evening.

"Cool contest, huh?" Tim asked.

"Cool isn't the word for it." Annie smiled with anticipation as she pulled her chair back around to her computer, erased Elvis once and for all, and tried to think romantic thoughts. "Romance Ambassador, here I come."

High above the streets of Manhattan, Zoë and Veronica Case-Dale were fighting over a copy of *Brat* magazine. *Brat* was their top fave, since it carried pictures of all the newest TV hunks, plus tons of ads for cool makeup and clothes. Browsing through *Brat* was almost as much fun as going to Bloomingdale's with their mother's credit card.

"Zoë!" Veronica tried again. "You've had it for *eons*. It's my turn now."

Without looking up, Zoë waved her younger sister away. "Chill out, Vern. I'll be done when I'm good and ready."

"Zoë!" Veronica moaned, throwing herself dramatically across the sofa, scattering all seventeen flowery chintz pillows in her wake. "It is *imperative* that I see that article on how to keep your boyfriend interested. I *need* to. Please, please, please?"

Zoë rolled her eyes. "You don't have a boyfriend, you dope."

"So?"

"No way."

"Way."

"No way."

Veronica sighed deeply. "What's so *momentous* anyway that you can't read faster?"

"A contest," Zoë allowed grudgingly. "I'm reading this ad for this contest."

"Get out! What stupid contest is so *crucial*?"

"A romance contest."

"Like you win a date with the guy on *Beverly Hills 90210*?" She grabbed the magazine to scan the page.

"Don't be a dweeb," Zoë shot back. At fourteen, she was frequently impatient with her eleven-year-old sister. "It's for these champagne guys. They want you to tell them about your romantic fantasy, and you could win a trip to Paris."

"Mom would never let us go to Paris."

"You don't know that for sure." Zoë tapped her chin with one finger. "I think we should enter."

"But, Zoë . . . I mean, what do we know about romance? Neither of us has ever even had a date."

"Oh, come on, you're always making up junk about guys on TV. Your stuff is better than any of the soaps."

"Well, yeah, but—"

"Don't sweat it, Vern. You always get A's on your essays at school, and you know more big words than anybody I know. So no prob—we make up something really steamy and we win the contest. And then," she finished up triumphantly, "Mom would have to let us go to Paris!"

"Yeah, well, look at the rules for a minute." Veronica held up the page. "Right there—'must be eighteen or older to enter.' So now what, Miss Not Even Fifteen?"

"So we'll lie about my age."

"We can't lie. We'd just get disqualified."

"So we'll enter under someone else's name."

"Yeah, like who?"

"Mom?"

"Right," Veronica snorted. "She would *annihilate* us."

Zoë scooted over to the couch, her eyes suddenly round. "What about Uncle Trevor?" She grabbed her sister's arm in excitement. "Vern, Vern, this is soooo perfect!"

"Uncle Trevor?" Veronica echoed doubtfully.

"Sure, sure. Listen a minute." Clearly in love with her idea, Zoë began to dance around a tufted Victorian footstool. "Remember that time with that model, what's-her-name, the one who got a divorce from

Johnny Scorch, the rock star? Uncle Trevor flew her to Morocco or Monsanto or whatever that place is where Princess Caroline lives—just for *dinner*, on a yacht. It's so perfect! We just pick Uncle Trevor's best date— if we pump Mom for details, we don't even have to make anything up—and we enter *him* in the contest!''

"It's Monaco, and besides, he flew her to Saint-Tropez, which is in France. *I* remember.'' Veronica's eyes narrowed. "I remember every *iota* of that *nefarious* seduction trip because he and that woman made the front cover of *Undercover USA*, and Mom called him up really steamed because she said he was ruining the family's reputation and he better stop or she was going to disown him. 'Just like a man, thinking with his hormones instead of his brain,' Mom said. 'I had to put up with this from my ex-husband, and I won't put up with it from you, too, even if you are my only brother and my only relative in the whole wide world.'''

"Mom can be such a drag.''

"Totally.''

"But hey, we don't even have to pump Mom, because you already know all the details! Nefarious seduction and everything—that sounds great.''

"Well, yeah . . .''

"So come on, Vern, let's go on Mom's computer, and you can write it and I'll help.''

"Well, maybe . . .''

On a roll, Zoë started dragging her sister down the hall. "This is going to be so cool, Vern. Wait till we win!''

A finalist. She could hardly believe it. Annie fished the official notification letter out of her briefcase for another look. Only four finalists, and she was one of them! Amazing. It was even more remarkable when she considered the fact that the other three finalists were definitely *somebodies*, and she was nobody with a capital *N*.

"So?" she asked herself blithely, trying to build up her bravado before she had to face her boss. "My entry clearly knocked their socks off because it was wonderful. Fabulous. Better than fabulous. The others got in because of who they are. I got in because of talent."

Of course, she had envisioned being given the Romance Ambassador position right off the top, so that she could waltz in and kiss her job good-bye. *Sorry, boss, but I am out of here!*

"It would have been nice," Annie whispered to no one in particular. Now, instead of making a dramatic exit from *Undercover USA*, she was going to have to proceed with caution. And lie through her teeth.

"I can't afford to lose this job before I'm sure about another one," she reminded herself as she walked carefully and calmly down the impossibly long hall to C. Todd Entwhistle's palatial office. She had too many bills to risk insulting the boss and going bankrupt in the process.

Meanwhile, there was the problem of what to tell old C. Todd to buy herself enough time to go to Paris and compete in the final round. She'd already used up her vacation, and she had no good reason to get emergency leave. She'd contemplated faking an appendicitis attack, but that was pretty lame.

Maybe, just maybe, there was a way to pull this off, with nobody the wiser. Thank goodness the letter from Framboise had given her an idea.

C. Todd was waiting when she got to the office. Overflowing the sides of a massive leather chair, he was puffing on a very large cigar and looking his usual unattractive self. His suits were always too loud, his hair too slick, and his body altogether too lumpy for the British gentleman look he thought proper for his position in life. What he looked like was a toad, and not surprisingly, C. Toad was what most of his staff called him.

"Hello, Mr. Entwhistle," she said quickly, banishing images of toads from her mind before she slipped up and called him that. Sliding into a chair, she tucked her skirt discreetly around her knees and got to the point. "I have a really exciting idea for an undercover story—me going undercover, I mean—on something called the 'Isn't It Romantic?' contest, sponsored by Framboise Champagne. I'd need to go to Paris for a week or two. No expense to the company, of course, because Framboise is picking up the tab."

"Why?" he asked, curling his lip.

C. Toad didn't believe in wasting words, so it was always tricky to pick through the conversation and divine exactly what he wanted to know. The nasty look on his face was a good hint, however, that this time he was demanding to be told, and pronto, under what theory a romance contest could possibly be of interest to *Undercover USA*.

"Celebrities," Annie said quickly.

"Who?"

"Well, Princess Kerenza, for one."

"Ahhh."

Annie hoped that cover possibilities were wafting through C. Todd's brain. Kerenza, a former Hollywood starlet who claimed to have married a Bulgarian prince somewhere among her fourteen or fifteen husbands, was flamboyant, outrageous, and always getting into scrapes. Her run-ins with police and presidents made great copy.

He raised one pencil-thin eyebrow. "And?"

"She's a finalist to be their romance spokesperson." Annie added slyly, "And so am I."

"How?"

"How did I get to be a finalist? I entered, under my maiden name, so they wouldn't connect me to *Undercover*." That much was true; she'd had a strong feeling the Framboise people wouldn't give her the time of day if they knew she worked for a tabloid. So, just on the off chance they might've remembered "Annie Porter" as a byline from a scandal sheet, she'd entered as "Anna Jonesborough," the girl she used to be.

"Maiden name?" His eyes flickered with interest. "I wasn't aware you'd ever been married."

"Oh, for about five minutes," she responded, wondering why he found the information interesting. "When I was young and foolish. Anyway, since my essay was good enough to get me a place as a finalist, it's a perfect opportunity to get inside the contest and get some dirt, don't you think?"

She was hoping against hope she'd get the Ambassador position, and never have to snoop for dirt again, but C. Toad didn't have to know that.

"Kerenza is always good for a line or two," he said expansively. He took a long drag on his cigar and then exhaled, blowing noxious smoke in a wide arc. "But not enough to justify sending you to Paris. Who else?"

"A romance novelist from Scotland—something MacDougal—the name is vaguely familiar. And Trevor Case."

C. Todd tried to sit up a bit. "*The* Trevor Case? The Legal Lothario? Casanova Case? Why didn't you say so? He's a lot better angle than that old tart Kerenza. He's hot, Porter—hot."

She hadn't mentioned him up front because she knew C. Toad would love going after him. Trevor Case was slick, gorgeous, a winner in court and out, and he dated more women than seemed humanly possible. Meanwhile, she wasn't at all sure she wanted to be within fifty miles of him. Casanovas made her crazy, and this guy was the king of Casanovas. Of course, Annie knew better than to believe what she read in *Undercover USA*. But still . . .

"All it says is, 'noted attorney Trevor Case.' I wasn't sure that was him," she said lamely.

"Of course it's him. This is good. Very good. Maybe a May-December fling with Trevor and Kerenza. Husband number twelve, perhaps?"

"I'm not sure focusing on Case is the right way to go—"

He waved a pudgy hand. "Don't be ridiculous. He sells."

"But he's such a—"

"No matter. We'll need pictures of Trevor and Kerenza together, or even better, him with Kerenza *and* the other one. We can get lots of mileage out of this." He giggled, giving Annie a quick glance. "Be nice to the man. Perhaps he'll find you the most interesting of the three. And wouldn't that be a scoop? 'I Was Casanova Case's Love Bunny—The Inside Story.'"

"I don't think so," she said sharply.

"Not your type?"

"Not by a long shot." She smiled grimly. "I despise lawyers. To a man, they're arrogant and insufferable. And I despise lover-boy lawyers even more."

"Was the late and unlamented Mr. Porter of that variety, perhaps?"

She was astonished that the old toad had figured it out so quickly. She'd have to remember to watch her step. He might be a toad, but he was a tricky one.

His phone rang, and the Toad dismissed her impatiently. "All set then. Keep us posted, Porter."

"Right."

As she wound her way back down the endless hallway, she comforted herself with the notion that she wouldn't really do any of it. And the deception would be worth it if she got to be the Romance Ambassador and never had to hear the name C. Toad Entwhistle again in her entire life.

Not far from her office, Tim was juggling several piles of envelopes and pushing the mail cart at the same time.

"Guess what," she called out. When he looked up, she announced brightly, "I'm going to Paris!"

* * *

Trevor Case was not a happy camper. "You did *what*?" he asked for the third time.

"It was Veronica's idea," one young niece said quickly.

"It was not!" the other one retorted. "You know good and well you started it, Zoë!"

Trevor held up both hands. "Stop it, please?" Nobody, but nobody, pushed Trevor Case around. So why was he so completely incapable of dealing with two little girls? "Both of you, sit down and be quiet," he ordered. "I have to think about this."

"Look, Uncle Trevor, it isn't so bad," Zoë began sweetly, batting her big brown eyes at him as she made no move to sit down or be quiet. "Just tell Mom you want to take us on a trip to Paris, for educational purposes or something dopey she'd believe. Then we can go, and you don't have to watch us, because Vern and I are totally capable of looking out for ourselves, and then we'll come home, and Mom will never know the difference!"

"We can't go," Veronica put in sensibly. "Mother already said we have to go to that stupid arts camp, and it's at the same time, and you know it."

"Gross. No TV, no phone, no nothing," Zoë complained. "Just a bunch of music and old paintings and boring stuff like that. Just think how much more educational Paris would be!"

"I can just imagine," he said severely. "But don't worry—you two aren't going to Paris. There is no way in he—" He was experiencing a dire need to curse a blue streak, but then these two little felons would probably start doing it themselves. Good grief. He was glad he wasn't their father. "There is no way possible your mother would ever let you go to Paris under my supervision." Zoë opened her mouth, and he moved to cut her off quickly. "*If* I were to agree to take you, which I wouldn't. You cheated and you lied, and I'm not going to encourage that kind of behavior by contemplating, for even three seconds, taking you to Paris. Not in this lifetime. So get that right out of your heads.''

''But, Uncle Trevor!'' Zoë wailed. ''We won! You can't take away our prize when we won fair and square.''

He glared at her, and she finally had the grace to sink to the sofa next to her sister. ''It was hardly fair *or* square, young lady.''

''So you're really not going to let us go?''

''I never wanted to go anyway,'' Veronica said in a trembling voice. ''It was all Zoë's idea, and it wasn't my fault at all, and I hope you realize that *Zoë* is the one who should be punished.''

''Punished?'' A tiny tear formed in the corner of Zoë's eye. ''Uncle Trevor, you aren't going to punish us, are you? Please, please, Uncle Trevor—don't tell Mom! You can't tell Mom!''

They were both staring up at him with such terrified expressions that he felt like an absolute ogre. Surely it was punishment enough that they wouldn't be allowed to go, without involving his uptight, semineurotic sister Constance in this mess. If he turned them over to Constance, they'd all be in for buckets of tears and recriminations.

Immediately the little con artists sensed the chink in his armor. ''You won't tell Mom, will you?'' they begged in unison.

''Don't press me,'' he said darkly.

''It was a really neat essay,'' Zoë ventured hopefully.

''And you always tell us that creativity is to be culti-vated,'' her sister added. ''It was very creative. Really.''

''I'll just bet it was.'' Trevor shook his head, feeling like a real marshmallow. ''Look, here's what I'll do. I won't tell your mother—'' As they whooped with joy, he continued, ''I won't tell your mother *if* you promise never to pull a stunt like this again as long as you live. Or at least as long as I live. Okay?''

"Promise," they chorused.

"Meanwhile, I'm going to have to go down to the Framboise office and explain that *we* are no longer an entry, that there was a mistake."

"Are you going to say we did it?" Veronica asked cautiously.

Trevor shook his head. "I don't think that's wise. Since you lied on the entry form, it might be construed as fraud, and I don't want to even raise the issue. No, I'll just tell them I changed my mind."

"But you get a free trip to Paris," Zoë reminded him. "Why don't you just take it?"

"Not on your life." He could just see himself as some cornball Romance Ambassador. Good grief. It was ludicrous. Not to mention embarrassing.

His partners at Chadwick & Case would have more than a few good laughs over that one, when he'd already provided enough entertainment to keep them occupied through the twenty-first century with the stories about his love life. He felt like punching a hole in a wall just thinking about it.

Of course, most of it was complete fabrication. It was true enough that he had a number of high-profile clients, and many of them were beautiful women. Once that was established, it was only natural to be seen out and about with them when they were working together on legal matters. But it didn't involve dating, and it certainly didn't involve sex.

Well, most of the time, anyway. And it was no business of those morons at *Undercover USA* if it did.

He was still smarting from the last "Casanova Case" article, linking him with a sultry Broadway star. "The Legal Lothario strikes again," it said, intimating that he had engineered the breakup of her marriage so he could handle her divorce. It didn't bother them in the least that he'd barely met the woman, and had never in his life handled a divorce case.

Ever since the damned article hit the stands, he'd

been inundated with copies of it. Stuck to his windshield, plastered all over his desk, even taped to the wall of his private restroom—the "Legal Lothario" lived on. It was infuriating, galling, and probably libelous. Now, if he only had time to get the papers together to file suit against that damned *Undercover USA* . . .

"Uncle Trevor, you look so mad," Veronica whispered. "We're really sorry. Aren't we, Zoë?"

"Forget about it," he said gruffly, reaching over to ruffle Veronica's hair. "I know where their offices are, so I'll go downtown right now and take care of this."

And if there was an *Undercover USA* cameraman lying in wait at the Framboise office, Trevor swore he'd strangle the jackass with his bare hands. "Casanova Case," he mumbled, pulling on his coat. "Good grief."

TWO

"You must be Mr. Case," the girl with the clipboard cooed. "You're late."

"Late? But I—"

"Right this way." Immediately she turned and swept down a maze of corridors decorated completely in pink. "Two of the other finalists are already here, so we just have to wait for Princess Kerenza and then we can get started."

"What do you mean, Princess Kerenza?"

"She's the fourth finalist." Jangling long earrings that looked like glitter balls on chains, the girl spun around long enough to give him an annoyed look from under her 1960s-style bouffant. "Didn't you read your letter?"

"I, uh, must have misplaced it."

She pointed a long, hot pink fingernail at a nearby door. "Just sit down in the reception room, and I'll be back later."

"Wait a minute," he called after her retreating back. "I need to speak to the person running this show—right away."

"You might just as well sit and wait like the rest of

us," a tall, slim redhead with a heavy Scottish burr said cheerfully from the doorway into the reception room.

He frowned at her. "Rest of whom?"

"The finalists, of course. There's me and you and the other one who's in there already."

He considered trying to find his way out of this place, but had to reject that idea. Too bad he hadn't thought to leave a trail of bread crumbs.

"Go on in and join the party," the redhead called out as she exited past him. "I'm just running to the loo and I'll be back in a jiff."

Giving up for the time being, Trevor ambled into the reception room. It, too, was a mass of pink, with rose-colored walls, mauve furniture, and showy lithographs of pink champagne and raspberries. He already felt like an idiot, and this Romance Ambassador thing hadn't even started. Folding his long frame into a dippy chair dripping in pink chintz, he didn't bother to pretend to be comfortable.

He glanced at the other occupant of the room—the other finalist—but she was hidden behind a travel magazine, and she made no move to lower it or introduce herself. All he saw were a great pair of legs in sheer black stockings and three-inch heels, the edge of a very short black skirt, and the top of her head. Small, sharp dresser, not friendly, he noted. But great legs.

They sat in silence, which suited him just fine, until the redhead came back. He couldn't have said what he expected a Romance Ambassador to look like, but he supposed this one fit the bill better than the unfriendly one, in a flaky sort of way. She looked like she had dressed haphazardly, with a gauzy dress tossed over leggings, and a big, floppy hat with the brim turned up in front. She just stood there in the doorway, staring at him with unabashed interest. When he decided to stare right back, she extended a hand.

"Jamesina MacDougal," she said loudly, in that rich Scottish accent. "I'm one of your fellow finalists. And you must be the one gentleman among us. Trevor Case, isn't it?''

"Yes, that's right.''

"When I saw your name on the sheet, I thought it was so familiar,'' Miss MacDougal mused. "But I can't for the life of me recall why.''

"Casanova Case,'' the other woman supplied from behind her magazine. "The Legal Lothario.''

"Only someone with very dubious reading habits would know that,'' Trevor returned, in his most ominous voice, guaranteed to squelch arguments from lesser souls. "Very dubious, as in *Undercover USA*. Are you fond of reading that brand of trash?''

The travel magazine snapped down, and a pair of blue eyes sent flaming arrows his way. "If you didn't read the same *dubious* material, you wouldn't recognize it, Mr. Case.''

Good comeback. And in that moment, even considering the fact that she was probably an avid reader of the worst kind of tabloid, his interest was aroused.

The world was full of women who wanted to sleep with "Casanova'' Case, just to say they had. He couldn't turn them down fast enough.

The world was full of women who were willing to sleep with "Open-and-Shut'' Case, to barter their bodies for his legal skills. The whole idea made him ill.

But the world was not full of women who would argue with him, challenge him, give him as good as he gave. He realized suddenly that it had been a long time since anybody had bothered to throw him a zinger.

He took a moment to inspect his opponent, realizing full well that his leisurely appraisal would only annoy her more. Her hair was blond and perfectly straight, chopped off chin length. The severe haircut looked just right with her small, delicate features, and those china blue eyes. Very pretty. Not overwhelmingly so, but pretty nonetheless.

Also not very tall—five-foot-one maybe, no more

than five-two. Her skirt was too short to be strictly business, and her taxi yellow and black blazer told him she wasn't afraid to stand out in a crowd.

He smiled. He had her number, all right. Small, feisty, dressed to kill. And she had already decided she hated his guts. What fun.

"Do I know you?"

"No," she returned. "Is that a variation on 'Haven't we met somewhere before?'"

"No."

"What a relief."

"You know, I feel I should point out that it's considered customary to be on more than a nodding acquaintance before hurling insults. But of course, those who read *Undercover USA* instead of Miss Manners are unlikely to be aware of that."

She crossed her arms over the front of her snappy little suit, and gave him a lethal glare. "My manners have nothing to do with it."

"Your manners are nonexistent."

"So are yours."

"Ah, the old 'ditto' comeback. Not very clever."

"Clever enough."

"For what?"

"To beat you at this contest, for one."

"I'd almost forgotten the contest."

She smacked her magazine down on the nearest mauve table. "How they could name you a finalist, I'll never know. The Legal Lothario, indeed. As if someone like you would know the first thing about romance."

"Someone like me?"

"Only takes clients he wants to date—only dates clients he wants to take. Isn't that what they say about you?"

"Not only are you foolish enough to read *Undercover USA*, but you compound the felony by actually believing it," he said darkly.

"What I do or don't believe is none of your business, Mr. Case." But she had a small, smug smile, and a touch of mischief lit her eyes.

His own eyes narrowed in her direction. And suddenly he knew that all this chitchat about his personal life was just a smoke screen. She was too smart to believe it, even for one minute, and they both knew it. He measured her with a level gaze, trying to figure out what her game was.

Her pointy little chin rose as she stared right back. Oh, yes, he knew without a doubt, he was absolutely right about her. Something was going on here. But what?

What was the real reason for her hostility? Maybe it wasn't Casanova Case, but Open-and-Shut Case, who bothered her. This was, after all, a contest, and maybe she was planning on winning it.

As nearly as he could remember from the sketchy information the girls had given him, there was no big money involved, no cars or furs or sweepstakes prizes. All you got was a trip to Paris, and a chance at a job as some sort of glorified spokesperson for the Framboise company. It sounded like being Miss America on a champagne theme. Definitely nothing he was interested in. But maybe his feisty little adversary was more interested than he was. Maybe the chance to be a Romance Ambassador was important to her, and she was afraid he was too tough to take on.

"I guess my reputation for winning precedes me," he said with a sly smile of his own. "What is it they say? My win-loss record is better than—"

"Better than Perry Mason and the Chicago Bulls combined," she finished for him. "Isn't that it?"

His smile grew wider, more self-satisfied. "Afraid of the competition?"

There was a pause. "I don't like you, Mr. Case."

"You don't know me, Miss . . ." He raised an eyebrow. "Who are you, anyway?"

"She's Anna Jonesborough," the redhead tossed in, waving her copy of the finalist letter for clarification. Both of them turned to find the source of the intrusion, but the woman just grinned. "Don't mind me. Get right back to your squabble, why don't you? I'm enjoying the sparks, personally."

"Sparks?" they exclaimed in unison.

"I happen to be a romance novelist," Jamesina Mac-Dougal confided. "I write this sort of thing all the time. They meet—sparks are flying every which way. Next thing you know—boom—it's happily ever after. Isn't it romantic?"

"Romantic?" the feisty blonde echoed. "It's disgusting."

Appropriately enough, Princess Kerenza chose that moment to make her entrance.

"Hello, all!" she announced blithely, sailing into the room like a grand ocean liner, trailing clouds of perfume in her wake. "The princess has arrived."

Beaming, she gazed down at them, as if anticipating hand-kissing or boot-licking. Dark and dramatic-looking, she was also more than a bit plump. But she clearly liked her body the way it was, or she wouldn't have been displaying quite so much of it. What there was to her dress was low-cut and frothy, in the same rosy shade as the reception room. Trevor reassessed his notion of the Romance Ambassador. This was it—with arrows and exclamation points.

The girl with the bouffant huddled somewhere behind the princess's flounces. "If you'll follow me," she shouted, "Mademoiselle Carnot will see you now."

"Trevor, darling," the princess breathed. With a grip that would've done a stevedore proud, she hauled him up next to her. "Won't you escort me?"

"Have we met?"

"In spirit, darling."

"Ah." He had no intention of becoming Princess Kerenza's boy-toy, not even for five minutes. "Well,

I think I'd just as soon go unescorted, if it's all the same to you."

The princess shook a finger at him, as if to say, *You naughty boy*, but she let herself be ushered out into the hall and down to another small reception room. This one was even pinker than the last, if possible, with a rather overpowering raspberry-vine wallpaper.

Four chairs—upholstered in the same raspberry print—flanked one side of a long table, while a pale, thirtyish woman in a bright fuchsia suit stood on the other, wearing a pained smile. The room was empty except for the chairs and a neat stack of papers in the middle of the table.

"Hello," the pale woman said, speaking so softly and carefully that Trevor wondered if she had a headache and didn't want to compound it. "I am Marie-Ange Carnot, vice president of Framboise Champagne."

"Marie-Ange, darling!" the princess cried, tripping over to the other side of the room to kiss the air in the general direction of the other woman's cheeks.

"Yes, of course, Princess Kerenza. So lovely to see you again."

Trevor noted the little exchange. So the portly princess already knew the Framboise people. From jet-setting, perhaps? Or because she was trying to get a head start in the contest? Glancing over, he caught a very speculative look on the face of Ann Whatever Her Name Was. She must be thinking the same thing he was thinking, and not appreciating it, either, in her obvious quest to be Numero Uno in the contest.

Meanwhile, Mademoiselle Carnot managed another strained smile and motioned for them to sit in the chairs opposite her. As they took their seats, she continued to stand, clasping her hands in front of her, maintaining a stiff, formal posture.

Taking the chair on the end, Trevor managed to grab Ann's elbow and yank her down next to him. Anything to keep him out of Princess Kerenza's range. The feisty little blonde gave him a scathing look, but she didn't say anything, merely fixing her eyes straight ahead at the woman from Framboise.

"I have flown here from our main office in Paris," Mademoiselle announced, "to congratulate all of you on having emerged victorious in the Framboise 'Isn't It Romantic?' contest. We have some minor paperwork for the four of you to complete—releases and so forth—and then we will be all set for our flight to Paris on the Concorde two weeks from today."

"The Concorde?" Trevor sat up at attention. "In two weeks?"

"Mr. Case lost his letter," the girl with the bouffant said sourly. "He doesn't seem to know what's going on."

Mademoiselle Carnot dismissed the matter as a trifle with one wave of her hand. "Quickly, a copy for Monsieur Case."

"It's not necessary," he broke in. "But I would appreciate an opportunity to speak with you privately about the contest. Then perhaps some of this—" he gestured at the release forms on the table "—can be avoided."

"Privately? Oh, no, no." Rosy color stained the woman's pale cheeks. "I am sorry, Monsieur Case, but privacy between you and me, well, it is impossible— against the rules, improper—you understand?"

Damn it anyway. Trevor clenched his jaw and rose to his feet. The uptight Frenchwoman was behaving as if she thought he was going to try to seduce his way into winning the contest if he had a few minutes alone with her! All because of that damned Casanova Case nonsense, no doubt. Was there anyone who hadn't read that junk?

With steely control, he placed both hands flat on the table. "It will save your company and your contest a lot of trouble if you will allow me to *speak* with you privately for approximately thirty seconds. You'll hear me out, mademoiselle, if you're wise."

He could see she wasn't pleased about it, but finally she pointed to the corner of the room and allowed, "A few seconds, monsieur. No more."

Already putting together the skeleton of his opening argument, he followed her over to the damned corner. At this point, he was seething that they'd made him wait, irritated that they'd thrown him up against a female barracuda while he waited, and furious that Mademoiselle Carnot didn't feel he could be trusted not to play footsie for the length of a five-minute conversation.

He had been known to barbecue his opponents on a spit when he was angry, and he was good and angry now.

What in the world was going on over in the corner?

Annie chewed her lip and tried not to stare. Old Open-and-Shut Case was fit to be tied, that much was obvious, while that cranky Carnot woman didn't look much better. They'd been over in the corner gesticulating and whispering at each other for a good five minutes, leaving the other three finalists to cool their heels.

So what was Trevor Case up to?

At first Annie had suspected him of angling for some advantage, but as hot under the collar as both of them appeared, that didn't seem too likely.

But then, she was having a hard time figuring him out in general. He was as gorgeous and as slick as he looked on the pages of the tabloids, and then some, but he didn't seem nearly as mean. She'd pictured him as a win-at-all-costs shark, the quintessential hired gun.

The articles about him—a few of which she'd written herself—painted him as a legal eagle with one, and only one, thing on his mind. Winning. He didn't care who his clients were as long as they paid, and paid well. He'd eked out an acquittal for a conniving TV evangelist, and then found loopholes for half a dozen slimeballs implicated in the S & L bailout. And then there was the Wall Street financier charged with insider trading. Open-and-Shut Case had won every single one of them.

How could he be so good at what he did unless he was a consummate jerk? Funny, he didn't seem like a jerk at all.

In person, he almost seemed sort of vulnerable. Her gaze swept back over him. No, that was impossible. Arrogant, definitely. Temperamental, maybe. Even grouchy. But not vulnerable.

He'd been positively nasty when she brought up his lover-boy reputation. Okay, so she hadn't been all that kind herself, but still . . . she would've guessed Trevor Case was too cool to bother with a few minor insults.

Speaking of cool, what was he doing in this contest, anyway? He didn't seem the right type at all, either to want the job or to go for a trip to Paris on a whim. No, he struck her as the whimless type entirely. Maybe it was part of his win-at-all-costs philosophy.

But here he was, arguing with the woman running the contest, as if he didn't care that he was wrecking his chances to win. So what did it all mean?

Annie cast another glance into the corner, narrowing her eyes at the dashing figure of Trevor Case. Tall, intense, beautifully groomed, with dark hair and steely gray eyes, he was the kind of man every woman drooled over. Every woman except Annie Porter, of course.

She didn't like lawyers. As a matter of fact, she absolutely loathed lawyers. Even taking that into account, there was something extra about Trevor Case that really raised her hackles. She didn't exactly know why, but the very fact of his existence seemed to tick her off. The idea of that existence going on in the same room made her want to kick him. Or at least tear his clothes off and bite him somewhere on that gorgeous body.

Inappropriate, she told herself severely. But she couldn't resist another peek back into the corner, as she pondered exactly where she'd take her nip if she had her way with Mr. Case.

"*Mais non*, you may not!" Marie-Ange suddenly shouted, and Annie jumped, immediately feeling guilty, as if the words were directed at her secret thoughts. She tried to hold back a tattletale blush.

Although Marie-Ange hadn't had much of an accent before, she sounded very French all of a sudden. "You have entered the contest, monsieur, and you have been chosen. We have already released the names to the press! You are the only man! With whom would I replace you at this late date? I don't care if you have changed your mind. It is too late! Change all you want—the rules say there will be four finalists, and *there will be four*! And one of them will be *you*!"

As if she'd only now realized how loudly she was speaking, Mademoiselle became flustered and backed away from Trevor Case. "Excuse me," she mumbled. "I will return after a moment." And then she scuttled out of the room before the others had a chance to speak.

Trevor Case just stood there, with his hands in his pockets, looking like a thundercloud, while the princess and Jamesina pretended to be interested in the pile of release forms. Annie felt no such compunction. She wanted to know what the heck was going on.

Casually she ambled over to where he was standing. She arched an eyebrow and said softly, "Why, Mr. Case, it sounds as if you don't intend to join us for the contest. Is there a problem?"

"I don't think that's any of your business," he said precisely, coldly.

"Well, Marie-Ange was certainly in a dither, wasn't she? But then, I guess you're used to that. You generally reduce your opponents to quivering lumps of jelly, don't you?"

When he didn't rise to the bait, Annie smiled sweetly. She knew she was being snide, and probably very foolish, but she couldn't resist. It was so much fun getting under his skin.

Echoing his words from their earlier conversation, she asked, "What's the matter, Case? Afraid of the competition?"

There was a dangerous pause.

"Afraid of *you*, Annie?" His voice was low and silky, and very wicked. "Not in this lifetime."

The gall of the man, calling her Annie, as if he knew that's what she preferred. Well, not from him. She said defiantly, "I think you're right to drop out. You haven't got a prayer of winning."

"I don't need prayer. I'm good enough without it."

"You insufferable, arrogant excuse for a—" she began, but broke off when Marie-Ange came careening back into the room.

"We have wasted enough time," the woman announced, giving them both a quelling stare. "Let's get started on the paperwork, shall we?"

"Coming, Case?" Annie asked. "Or are you still planning to fold your tents and run away?"

Edging in front of her, Trevor Case strolled back to his chair, forcing her to practically climb over him to get to her own seat.

"Bring on the release forms," he said smoothly. "Looks like we're going to Paris."

THREE.

Annie ducked her head and lugged her carryon bag behind her. She tried to quell the butterflies in her stomach, but it was dicey.

For one thing, she wasn't a good flyer. The prospect of strapping herself into a seat and launching herself into space always unnerved her. It didn't help that the Concorde was much smaller than she'd expected. Surely a plane that swept through the sky faster than the speed of sound ought to be huge and powerful and overwhelming, as a buffer against falling into the ocean. Instead, it looked fragile and very scary, like a skinny little duck. A lame duck.

She swallowed and tried to focus on something else. But if she didn't think about the plane, her mind immediately returned to Trevor Case. The concept of "butterflies" didn't begin to capture what Trevor Case did to her. Luckily, he hadn't boarded yet, and she didn't have to look at him while her brain reminded her of the devastating, infuriating impression Mr. Big Shot had made. She could feel her blood pressure rise just thinking of him.

It isn't your blood pressure you're worried about, she thought gloomily. It was all the rest of her traitorous

34

senses, the ones that kept begging her to trace the chis-
eled line of his jaw, to stare deep into the storm-tossed
gray of his eyes. She'd been down that road before,
with someone who wasn't nearly as smart or as charis-
matic or as downright *mind-boggling* as Trevor Case.
And she'd certainly regretted that bit of folly, hadn't
she? No, she was going to have to put Case and his
charms out of her mind, or risk flying home from Paris
penniless, jobless, lonely, and *very* cranky.

"No way," she said out loud, squaring her shoulders
and moving purposefully down the aisle.

Framboise had taken over the entire first-class section
for its VIP passengers, and first class on this plane was
pretty impressive. In fact, it looked like someone had
redecorated just for this flight, since the seats and the
walls were covered with the familiar raspberry pink
print. Or maybe this was the company Concorde. Who
knew? Whatever the answer, Annie began to feel more
like the royalty the contest brochure had promised.

Speaking of royalty, Princess Kerenza was blocking
the whole aisle as she squeezed herself around Marie-
Ange and into the window seat in the first row. It was
a clear effort to monopolize Marie-Ange, the only
member of Framboise brass available, for the entire
flight. Annie glared at the princess's ample rear end as
it wedged itself into place.

As she scoped out the rest of the first-class section,
deciding where it would be most politic to sit, a silky
voice murmured in her ear, "Well, if it isn't our little
Annie."

Trevor Case had arrived. Not only that, but he'd
sneaked up on her from behind when she wasn't looking. As his warm breath tickled her ear, Annie's whole
body ricocheted onto red alert. She felt herself begin
to tingle from head to toe.

Quickly she took control, absolutely refusing to let
him throw her for a loop. She lifted her chin and turned
on him.

"Our little Annie?" she asked with distaste. It sounded like Little Orphan Annie. She'd put on a bright red power suit for this trip, and she had no intention of feeling like a child.

Besides, he had no reason to toss nicknames at her. As far as everyone connected with the contest knew, she was down-home Anna Jonesborough, not cynical, jaded tabloid maven Annie Porter.

She had a momentary jolt of panic as she pondered the suspicious fact that he was calling her by her real nickname. Maybe he'd called her Annie because he knew what she was up to. Maybe he wasn't fooled for one minute by her sneaky resumption of her maiden name just to get safely into the contest. Maybe he recognized her as Annie Porter, secret agent for *Undercover USA*. If he knew, and he shared his information with the Framboise people, her goose was cooked.

It was enough to make her want to chew on her newly polished nails. But no, he couldn't know, she realized with relief. If he did, he'd be using it against her, not breathing in her ear.

She purposely bonked her carryon bag into his shin as she took a few steps away from him. What was he up to? Ruthless and cunning, Trevor Case was a master manipulator who played on juries' sympathies as expertly as Itzhak Perlman played the violin. So what game was he playing now?

"Where are you sitting?" he asked casually.

Annie narrowed her gaze. She had the distinct feeling he would slide his long, lean, *unwanted* body right up next to whatever seat she chose. Quickly she ducked into the aisle seat next to Jamesina MacDougal, who was gazing out the window in row three. Take that, she thought triumphantly. Now there was no empty seat next to her for the predatory lawyer to fill.

But he gave her an enigmatic smile and settled in right across the aisle. She pulled out the diagram of the airplane, concentrating on flotation devices to be used in case of crash, but she knew he was still watching her.

Why? Why was he tormenting her like this? It was almost as if he were pursuing her, just to make her squirm.

After all, he could hardly be legitimately interested, in a normal man-to-woman way. Not that she'd have gone for him anyway, but she might at least have been flattered. But the chances of him actually, genuinely, verifiably getting hot for her were infinitesimal.

She shook her head. There was simply no way. Annie Porter, who hadn't had a date in over a year, couldn't attract flies, let alone Mr. World Class Bachelor About Town.

"Not even in my league," she whispered under her breath. She was hardly the high-society, uptown type he preferred, if the stories about him were to be believed. She reminded herself that, of course, she knew better than anyone not to believe what she read in the newspaper. But still . . . the image of Trevor Case arm in arm with some impossibly gorgeous model or actress wouldn't go away.

Looking very festive in a pink suit with a Framboise pin winking on her lapel, the flight attendant was pouring liberal doses of the home brand of champagne, and Annie accepted one to be social. Distracted, she took a sip or two as she considered the issue of Trevor Case.

She'd seen his face plastered across the pages of her very own paper, linked with the loveliest of the lovely—high-fashion models, beauty queens, even a female senator! On this one plane, he had the choice of Jamesina, the flaky romance novelist; Kerenza, the curvaceous, exotic princess; or Marie-Ange, a top exec from a multinational corporation. He belonged with the sort of woman who spent her free time in mudpacks at Elizabeth Arden, the sort of woman who was dressed and coiffed within an inch of her life.

So what would he want with a five-foot-tall loud-mouth who cut her own hair with manicure scissors?

No, there was something very suspicious about Mr. Case's interest. Suddenly Annie felt sure it all centered around the contest. Perhaps old Open-and-Shut Case wanted to rack up another victory, and this flirting stuff was part of his master plan to distract Annie. If he'd scoped her out as the main competition, what better way to neutralize her than to romance and confuse her? It made a weird sort of sense. . . .

But the plane jolted down the runway, spilling her champagne, and she forgot anything except the fact that she was once again defying gravity and tempting fate.

She was halfway through her familiar litany of prayers to whatever higher being was listening, just ready to launch into "If you let me get through it this time, I promise never ever to fly again as long as I live," when Jamesina patted her hand and interrupted the flow.

"Your first flight?" she asked kindly.

"No, I've done it a million times," Annie said grimly. "But it never gets any better."

Trevor angled his long legs out into the aisle and leaned into the conversation. "A good belt of Scotch will take care of it."

"I don't use alcohol to deaden my senses," she said primly. She glanced down at the fat raspberry sitting all by itself at the bottom of her champagne glass, recalling what she'd drunk and who her sponsor was a bit too late. "Not Scotch, anyway," she amended quickly.

"Oh, I don't think your senses need deadening," he offered, in that same cool, infuriating voice. "Personally, I prefer a woman who's alive and kicking."

There was something extremely sexual about the way his silky voice lingered on the words. She could feel her ears burning, but she had no intention of following up on it. Instead, she buried herself in the emergency instructions, checking out just where the closest exit would be in case she needed it. To really insulate herself from the annoying Mr. Case, she stuck on a pair of headphones. Meanwhile, the handy flight attendants were bringing the champagne around again. She took another glass and tossed it back defiantly.

Eric Clapton came over her earphones, and she turned it up louder. It was a soft song, something sexy and a little rough, the kind of thing she could imagine dancing to, very slow and very close. She swallowed. Romantic fantasies were not what she needed with Eric Clapton in her ear and Trevor Case practically sitting in her lap.

"Prickly little thing, isn't she?" Case shouted across her, smiling amiably at Jamesina as if Annie were unable to see or hear him. Too bad she could see and hear him just fine. It wasn't possible to crank up the airline music loud enough to block him out.

"I expect it's just the flying," the Scottish woman said helpfully.

Trevor angled farther into the aisle, his foot almost touching hers as he commented sagely, "Oh, really?"

Jamesina shrugged. "We all have our irrational fears. Mine's spiders. Can't abide the things. What's yours?"

"I don't know. I guess I'm fearless," he said with a laugh.

Annie steamed, stuck in the middle of this inane conversation. Who cared about Scottish spiders? And who couldn't have guessed that Trevor would claim to be courageous beyond all belief? "Hmph," she muttered. "Fearless, my foot."

"Did she say something?" he inquired. "Jamesina, you're sitting closer than I am. Did you hear something?"

"Please, call me Jamie. No, I didn't hear a word."

Trevor smiled, flashing perfect white teeth in a dangerously beautiful smile. "You know," he said gallantly, "you do look more like a Jamie than a Jamesina. I should've guessed."

Annie burned. Meanwhile, Trevor's new best pal Jamie leaned farther into the armrest in her attempt to carry on this scintillating conversation, while Trevor kept encroaching from the aisle. Annie leaned back into her seat as far as she could go, but it wasn't far enough. Not nearly far enough.

Jamie was actually the closer of the two, but all Annie cared about was the onslaught on her senses coming from the other side. Trevor's side.

She caught the scent of clean man and a hint of cologne, something elegant and subtle that barely teased her nose. Expensive and devastating, just like the rest of him. She could smell him, she could breathe him, she could feel him. She could almost taste him. . . .

Her hands clenched around the emergency brochure as she squashed herself down into her seat. There was no way she was going to give him the satisfaction of reacting to him and his stupid games.

In her ears, the Fine Young Cannibals were rolling through "She Drives Me Crazy." Losing one small *S*, Annie could relate. In spades.

Finally she was at the end of her rope. She'd had enough of being pushed around, talked over, and breathed on. "Excuse me," she said tightly, removing her headphones and rising from her seat.

"Is something wrong?" Trevor asked innocently.

"Perhaps Jamie and I should change seats," Annie suggested from between clenched teeth. "Then you two could have your chat without the barrier in between."

"I'm fine," Trevor said cheerfully. "How about you, Jamie?"

"Just fine," she hastened to assure them. "I'm enjoying sitting next to Annie."

Right. Annie mumbled something about the ladies'

room as she maneuvered her way over Trevor's legs and out into the aisle. She couldn't think or even breathe stuck there like that, like a bug with its wings pinned to a collector's board.

She was only planning to go to the rest room and splash some cool water on her face. But as she passed the first row and spied Marie-Ange, she remembered the little altercation Case and the Frenchwoman had gotten into. And then, without warning, a really dirty trick just popped into her head.

She hesitated to go ahead with it. She might work for *Undercover USA*, but she did have her standards. Nevertheless, a quick glance back at Trevor, still way out into the aisle, still happily exchanging chitchat with Jamie, convinced her. He deserved it. And if the tables were turned, she felt sure Mr. Open-and-Shut Case would have no qualms about sabotaging her.

"Marie-Ange, can I speak with you for a moment?"

"Certainly," Mademoiselle Carnot replied with a sigh of relief. She began to stand, but Princess Kerenza immediately launched into a protest.

"Marie-Ange, Marie-Ange!" she cried. "You haven't heard what happened *after* Maurice Chevalier sent me fifteen dozen roses!"

"Later," Mademoiselle Carnot shot back, with a definite edge to her voice. "I shall hear it later."

Marie-Ange stood up abruptly and, with the princess still quibbling behind her, led Annie down the aisle. "We may speak here," she said, ducking into the tiny galley area of the plane. "I must thank you for the interruption, Miss Jonesborough. Princess Kerenza can be . . ." She broke off, wiping her brow. "Excuse me."

Annie offered the Frenchwoman her most sympathetic smile. "Oh, it's quite all right," she said quickly. "I understand. In fact, I understand only too well."

"Excuse me? Princess Kerenza has also . . . ?"

"No, no, not her. Him." She inclined her head in Trevor's direction.

"The princess is bothering him as well?"

"No." She paused. "At least not that I know of." At Marie-Ange's look of complete confusion, Annie explained, "*He's* the one who's bothering *me*. You see, he's . . ." She manufactured shame and distress, with just the right touch of dignity.

"What has he done?" Marie-Ange asked solicitously, and Annie knew she'd hooked the woman.

Now to reel her in. "It's very embarrassing, mademoiselle. I'm afraid I have to ask you to disqualify him from the contest."

Marie-Ange's eyebrows shot up so far, they were in danger of disappearing altogether. "Dis—dis—qualify? *Mais non! I cannot! C'est impossible!*"

Annie concentrated on mastering her woebegone expression. At this point, she felt less was probably more in terms of comment on her part.

"What has he done that is so terrible?" Marie-Ange demanded.

"Well, you know about his reputation, Casanova Case and all that?"

Mademoiselle's cheeks grew very pink. "Yes, I have heard about this."

"Let me simply say, he deserves it," Annie whispered in a meaningful tone.

"He has bothered you?"

"Oh, yes." She knew she was being very wicked, but there was no turning back now. "And now he's hassling Jamesina."

After a quick peek down the aisle, Marie-Ange looked less convinced. "She doesn't look so hassled to me."

"Well, she is. And after her, who will be next? Princess Kerenza? And then you yourself, mademoiselle?" She sniffed. "It's disgraceful. The man is a menace."

"Yes, I think so, too," Marie-Ange muttered. "He is altogether too sure of himself, too masculine, too . . . pushy, yes?" She shook her head. "I know his type, Miss Jonesborough. I was married to his type. It's not good."

"You, too?" Annie was stunned. "I was married to one of those, too. Yours wasn't a lawyer, was he?"

Marie-Ange patted her new compatriot's hand. "No," she said with spirit. "Race-car driver. Beautiful man, you understand, but his ego, his arrogance." She raised her eyes skyward. "Impossible."

"Exactly," Annie said with spirit. "So you will disqualify him?"

"But how can I? We are in the middle of the ocean, Miss Jonesborough. Would you have me toss him overboard?"

"Well, no, but once we get to Paris, surely you can send him home? I mean, he tried to get out, didn't he? Back in New York, I mean?"

"Yes, he did, but it was impossible then, and it remains so."

"But he's driving me bananas!"

"I'm very sorry," Marie-Ange offered, shaking her head. "I would help you if I could. I will admit to you that I am not happy he is here. Monsieur Case's essay was not as strong as yours or Miss MacDougal's, but he is a man. Our president was enchanted with the idea of at least one man as a finalist, and a man of Monsieur Case's stature . . . Well, it was irresistible. I'm sure you understand."

"Oh, I understand." Annie had been in the real world long enough to know that talent, intelligence, being a nice person——none of that was worth a red cent. To succeed in this life, you had to have an angle. And Trevor had so many angles, he could've taught geometry. For him, of course the sponsors would stretch and cheat. She scowled. "So no matter what, he's in?"

"I'm afraid so. We have already released the names and invited the members of the press to come and view the fantasies. He is an important man, a big draw, yes?"

"Yes." Annie chewed her lip. "Okay, so you can't disqualify him. But you might be able to scare him enough to get him to behave."

"Scare him?" Marie-Ange echoed doubtfully.

"Exactly." Annie smiled. "Here's what you say. . . ."

Trevor was enjoying himself. For some reason he couldn't quite figure out, he thought it was fun to bother Annie. Sort of like dipping little girls' pigtails in inkwells. After she'd stomped off like that, he knew she was clearly feeling the impact of his campaign.

But then she swept back into her seat, looking unconcerned and smug. Immediately his alarms rang. If he read her correctly (and he was very good at deciphering people's underlying motives), she thought she'd won a round.

And he didn't know why yet. One of his best skills was staying a step ahead of the opposition. He'd research all night long, he'd sweat over strategy and tactics, he'd obsess over every little detail rather than risk missing something.

As a matter of fact, he despised surprises. And right now, he had the definite feeling that Little Miss Annie had a surprise up her sleeve.

Waiting for opening shots from that direction, he wasn't prepared when Mademoiselle Carnot stopped at his elbow, wearing a chilly expression.

"Monsieur Case, I must speak with you," she announced. Without pausing for a response, Marie-Ange wheeled and stalked into the almost empty coach section of the airplane.

Trevor didn't want to, but he followed. Across the

aisle, Annie's smile widened, just like the Cheshire cat. He didn't like the looks of this at all.

Marie-Ange seemed very nervous as she pointed to a seat, and then stood next to him. "It has come to my attention that you are not behaving yourself, Monsieur Case. This will not continue."

"Behaving myself?" It sounded like Tom Brown's School Days. Trevor smiled. "Behaving myself?" he repeated.

"Exactly. It must stop. You will not bother the other contestants, or I will take action."

Bothering the other contestants, huh? He could guess precisely where that came from—Little Miss Annie had tattled on him. That much he could believe, but Marie-Ange's reaction was a bit much. Why in the world had she decided to dress him down like a naughty kid caught with a cookie jar? Didn't she realize she was skating on thin ice?

"And what sort of action are you proposing, if I don't choose to *behave myself*?" he asked lazily. "You won't kick me out—you can't."

"Don't be so sure—" she began, but he cut her off.

"We both know I tried to back out peacefully at the beginning, and you refused to let me go. My only conclusion is that you need me in this contest for some reason. My high profile, perhaps." He gave her a crooked smile. "Therefore, it would behoove you to be nice to me, mademoiselle, so that I don't go away and leave you in the lurch."

"Don't threaten me, Monsieur Case," she said awkwardly. She raised a limp hand to her forehead. "I will not be pushed by you, do you understand?"

"You don't have a choice." He stood to go, at the end of his patience with Mademoiselle Carnot's trumped up nonsense.

But the lady kept talking. "It would not be so good for your reputation if, very quietly, with much distress, I were to disqualify you when we got to Paris. I would give no reason for the disqualification, of course, but I might perhaps hint to the press the idea that there was something underhanded about your behavior, and that we couldn't possibly keep you as a contestant.''

Was he being paranoid, or was she really implying that she would spread a rumor that he'd been caught cheating? As in entering under false pretenses. As in letting his nieces fill in his name, and going along with it. Trevor felt a twinge of unease. Nobody knew about his juvenile delinquent nieces, he felt sure. But if somebody started nosing around, like checking signatures, for example, he and the girls could be in big trouble. But he simply couldn't believe that Marie-Ange had those kinds of suspicions.

No, she was just bluffing; he was sure of it. Knowing that he was a prominent attorney, with a reputation to protect, the Frenchwoman had taken a shot in the dark, hoping that her vague allusions to ''something underhanded'' would keep him under wraps.

He turned. ''You're not going to disqualify me,'' he said softly. ''That's a given.''

''I could tell a few friends in the press that Monsieur Casanova is up to his old tricks,'' she blustered. ''Everyone has heard about you. Three women, one Casanova—it's a pretty picture, yes?''

He relaxed. Marie-Ange had no idea there was anything wrong—all she knew about was the stupid Legal Lothario rumors. ''And since it's a lie,'' he said calmly, ''I could sue you for every franc in the company till, Miss Carnot.''

Her face flushed with color. ''I want my contest to run smoothly, monsieur. You quit throwing the clog in the works, or we will both see what you push me to.''

He gave her the benefit of a dazzling smile. Empty threats. As he ambled back to first class, Trevor dismissed Marie-Ange and her paltry attempts to scare him without a second thought. But what really scorched him, from the soles of his feet on up, was Anna Jonesborough, bigmouth and troublemaker. He was going to have to neutralize that one.

"Don't worry. It didn't work," he told her as he bent down over her, trapping her in her seat.

She tried to wiggle away, but there was no place to go. "Excuse me?"

"I know you were behind it. You told her to play the Casanova angle." He smiled wickedly down at Annie. "You thought I'd get mad and walk. But it didn't work." He bent down closer, ruffling her hair with his breath. "I'm still here, and so are you."

"I don't know what you're talking about," she returned. "I think you've lost it, Mr. Case."

"I haven't lost anything, Annie." With his lips a fraction of an inch from her pretty pink ear, he whispered, "But you will, if you keep this up."

She shut her eyes and swallowed, and he knew she was fighting for control. *Too late, sweetheart.*

"I won't lose," she murmured.

"You already have."

With a muttered oath, she whipped off her seat belt and practically knocked him over in her haste to get out in the aisle. He knew it was on purpose when she trod down hard on his foot on the way out.

"You're really very mean to her," Jamie reproved him. She shook a finger at him. "You're perfectly polite to me, but very rude and very upsetting to poor little Anna."

He raised an eyebrow. "Poor little Anna?"

Jamie shrugged. "She seems very sweet, except around you, of course."

"What do you know about her, anyway?"

After a moment of poking around in her huge satchel of a purse, Jamie waved a letter at him. "All I know is what it says in the letter. You're Trevor Case, attorney, New York, New York. And she's Anna Jonesborough, journalist, Hixville, Illinois."

"Journalist? Is that what it says?"

"Yes, that's what it says." Jamie frowned at him. "I know the two of you are developing a major case of the hots for each other," she said calmly, as Trevor tried not to choke. "But this is going a bit too far, don't you think? This is more like, well, all-out war. Of course, I've written that, too, but . . ." She sighed. "I think you should be honest with her. Why not tell her you're feeling vulnerable, and are simply unaccustomed to dealing with such an immediate and overpowering attraction?"

Trevor stared. The most amazing part was that Jamie seemed completely serious. "I don't think so," he managed.

"Which part?"

"All of it. I'm not suffering from any 'overpowering attraction,' I can assure—"

"Poppycock," Jamie interrupted. "If you aren't attracted to her, then why are you so beastly?"

"Because she's a very strange person." Saying that to Jamie with a straight face wasn't easy. "And I think she's hiding something. In fact, I'm sure of it. She's trying to keep me on the defensive, so I won't look behind her offense. There's a weak link there, and that's what she's hiding."

"I haven't a clue what you're saying," Jamie protested, but Trevor was too far into his train of thought to stop to explain.

The more he thought about it, the more sure he became that he was right. Anna Jonesborough didn't add up. And if she wasn't what she seemed, then what was she?

"Excuse me," he told Jamie, snagging the letter from her hand and backing up into coach class again. He knew he'd find telephones built into the backs of the seats, and plenty of privacy while he made his suddenly important call.

"It's Case," he said when the investigator he always used picked up on the other end. Trevor wasted no time on pleasantries or other frills. "Female Caucasian, approximately twenty-five years old, five foot one, a hundred pounds. Name is Anna Jonesborough. She says she's a journalist from Hixville, Illinois." He paused. "What do I want? Everything. Everything you can find."

_____ TAILS OF THE CITY _____

_____ FOUR _____

Even if that beastly Trevor Case kept casting strange,
measuring glances her way, Annie tried to relax, to
enjoy the luxurious plane ride. Three or four more
glasses of that delightful champagne didn't hurt anything, of course. Her companions and her surroundings
took on a soft, romantic glow, as if she were flying
through the sky by candlelight.

At first she'd felt like she was out of her league
with this group of celebrities, but she tried to encourage
herself with a positive attitude. As far as the competition went, Annie decided that Jamie was too sweet and
nice for her own good, that Kerenza was an idiot who
couldn't be taken seriously, and that it was easy to
ignore ol' Trevor if she just concentrated. After all,
what would a mover and shaker like him want with a
Romance Ambassador job? Obviously he was only
doing it for a few laughs, a few days recreation. As
soon as things got tough, he'd go back to what he was
good at—being a shark in lawyer's clothing.

She did spare a few moments to wonder what Case
had been doing back in the coach section all that time,
making mysterious phone calls, but there was no way
to ask politely, so she squelched her curiosity with an-

other glass of cool, delectable champagne. Who cared what Case was up to?

He might be able to get by on slick good looks and personal charm in the courtroom, but *this* was a whole different ball game. "I can beat him," she whispered to herself. "He's a man. What do men know about romance?"

"What did you say?" Jamie asked.

"Nothing," she returned, with her most serene smile. She was just digging the last raspberry out of the bottom of her champagne flute when the announcement came to fasten seat belts.

Already feeling the usual airplane anxiety, even through her champagne-induced glow, Annie wrenched her seat belt around her waist as tightly as it would go without giving her a hernia, and then gripped her armrests with all her might. As the plane took a ferocious descent, sending her heart right up into her throat, she gritted her teeth and tried to think about happy things.

It wasn't working.

Engines that caught fire, wings that fell off, pilots who keeled over at the controls—images of death and disaster raced through her mind. She groaned, praying that it would all be over soon.

But then Trevor leaned across the aisle again, interrupting her fierce concentration on her imminent demise. "I'm curious, Annie— "

"I would prefer it," she said tightly, "if you wouldn't call me that."

"Too intimate for you?"

"Intimate?" she choked, feeling that last damn raspberry stick in her throat.

What was wrong with the man? Didn't he know how a word like "intimate" sounded in that silky, seductive tone of his? It sounded like very old whiskey poured over cracked ice, like . . . like satin sheets rustling over naked skin. It sounded like a whole lot of things she didn't want to think about at the moment.

With a great deal of effort, she pulled herself together, fanning her flushed cheeks with the emergency procedures flyer. "Nobody calls me Annie," she lied.

"Why not?"

The plane took a dip, and so did her stomach. And then there was an ominous rumble under her feet, as if something important were getting ready to fall off the plane. Like an engine. She let out a little yelp of fear, which she hoped no one heard. Talking to cover her quaking heart, she declared, "If I'm going to die within the next few minutes, I'd like to be called by my real name while I still have a chance."

But Case only smiled. "Annie," he said softly, pulling out the two small syllables, making it sound more like an endearment than a name.

"Don't," she warned him, but she knew he would.

"Annie," he repeated calmly, with the same long, drawn-out delivery. There was a curious, mischievous light dancing in his stormy gray eyes. She didn't like the looks of that at all. "What was your entry in the contest?"

"My what?" She was still trying to get over the way her name sounded on his lips, and she had no idea what he was talking about.

"Your romantic fantasy," he told her. "I've been mulling it over, and I can't imagine what someone like you would think up."

Her eyes widened, but she couldn't tear them away from his gorgeous face. His smoky voice sent little sparks and shivers down her spine, tripping alarms in an already overloaded nervous system, making it hard for her to breathe under her too tight seat belt.

"Don't tell me you're afraid to share it with me?" he asked, with a quirk of his narrow, mocking mouth.

Afraid? How about petrified? "I sent it to the Framboise people to broadcast to the world," she responded uneasily. "Why should I care if you know?"

She paused, stalling for time. When she'd been in

her office, all by herself, trying to think up something sexy and provocative, something so romantic and special it would capture the interest of the Framboise people, she'd let her imagination run away with her. But she hadn't anticipated what it would feel like to have to actually talk about it to someone else. Especially someone as arrogant and manipulative and downright confusing as Trevor Case.

Writing it down for herself and talking to *him* about it were very different matters. "Why do you want to know?" she asked suspiciously.

"Just curious," he said with a sly smile. "Why are you so afraid to tell me?"

"I'm not afraid. Not afraid at all." She chewed the tip of one nail, trying desperately to think of some way out of this dilemma.

"You definitely seem afraid to me," he said dryly.

"Of course not. It's just that, uh, I don't want to give anything away before the competition gets started," she improvised. "Maybe we're not supposed to. And who knows? Maybe you'll steal my idea or something."

"I don't believe that sort of theft is possible," Jamie put in kindly. "They have all of our fantasies on file, don't they? So we wouldn't be able to change things at the last moment. I mean, they'd know the fix was in, wouldn't they?"

"They have our essays on file?" Trevor had a very strange look on his face. His jaw was clenched, and his eyes were cloudy and speculative, as if he had suddenly realized something that gave him a great deal of concern.

Annie mused, "Obviously it bothers you that they have copies of our fantasies on file. But why?" An unsettling notion occurred to her, and she leaped headlong into the fray. "Unless you *were* planning on stealing from one of the rest of us. I was right, wasn't I?"

His expression was priceless. "You can't be serious."

"But I am. Perfectly serious."

He gave her a piercing stare. "I would never steal anyone else's idea, and you know it."

But did she? After all, Marie-Ange had indicated that Trevor's essay was nothing special, and that he'd reached finalist status only because he was famous and because he was a man. Maybe he knew his entry was a loser and he wanted to beef it up with bits of other people's ideas.

But no. With a shade of disappointment, Annie realized she didn't seriously believe he would filch her fantasy or anybody else's. For one thing, he was plenty smart enough to know that whoever he stole from would scream bloody murder. Besides, she couldn't imagine him committing petty thievery like that. He was arrogant and competitive, yes, but not a cheater. Gazing at him, getting a good, long look into those steady, confident gray eyes, she knew he firmly believed he could win any competition on his merits, without resorting to dishonesty.

Nonetheless, there was still something very fishy going on here. Normally, of course, she wouldn't have touched his fantasies with a ten-foot pole. She could just imagine what the Legal Lothario would think up—something sinfully expensive, something dark and dangerous and achingly sexy. . . .

Her mind created the scenario before she could stop it.

Trapped alone with a stranger in an elegant penthouse. Wet clothes. No lights. No heat. No power. Only each other and a case of chilled champagne.

Who cared if they were strangers? For this one moment in time, there'd be no excuses, no regrets. They'd light up the black night with their passion, wrapped desperately in each other's arms.

Annie closed her eyes and made a tiny moan just thinking about it. "Oh, my," she breathed.

But wait, that was *her* fantasy. Confused, she sat up straighter in her seat, primly clutching the armrests. She even turned the cool air jet above her head on full blast, but she still felt overheated.

Since when had Trevor Case shown up in her fantasy? That wasn't the way it was supposed to happen. She didn't even like him, and she certainly didn't want him playing her sexy stranger or doing any of the other rather erotic things her essay had outlined.

He was watching her intently, and his gaze seemed to hold her fast, trapping her in her seat, as if he knew exactly what she was thinking. Ignoring the rush of hot color flooding her cheeks, Annie did the only thing she could think of. She launched an offense of her own.

"So what was in *your* essay, Mr. Case?" she demanded. "Since there's some question here as to your integrity, I think you ought to put your own romantic fantasy out in the open, so we'll know whether you keep to it or not."

"Absolutely not," he said flatly, sending her a hard glare from under the dark slash of his brows.

"But why not?" She loosened her belt a little so she could turn more his way. She had Trevor Case on the defensive, and she saw no reason to let up now. Besides, if she heard his lukewarm fantasy with her own ears, it might douse the flames of her own hot little idea. "Come on, Case. Give."

"As a matter of fact, Miss Jonesborough," he returned coldly, "that essay is at the moment only a dim memory. I would need to review it, to refresh my recollection, before I could discuss it."

"Spoken like a lawyer." Instead of the silky lover's tones, she was getting Attorney for the Prosecution. At least she could handle this one a little better. "So go ahead—review all you want." She waved a breezy hand at his briefcase. "It was a maximum of five pages. How long can it take you to skim over that?"

"I didn't keep a copy of it."

Annie considered this new bit of information. Curiouser and curiouser. "Frankly, I'm shocked, Mr. Case. A man with your brilliant reputation having difficulty remembering the contents of a teeny, tiny thing like a five-page essay? And then you didn't bother to keep a copy? As I recall, you didn't have a copy of the finalist letter back in New York, either."

"You may be in trouble, Trevor," Jamie ventured. "The instructions said that we were supposed to stick to the letter of our original essays, and that Framboise wouldn't offer any help." She began digging through the papers in her own tote bag. "It says right here, 'You are responsible for bringing any materials you may need, as well as copies of your entry. Framboise personnel will provide assistance with routine matters pertaining to French sites and locations, but will not provide any entrant with duplicates of original entries, advice, or ideas.' "

Annie raised a pale eyebrow. "You're not going to be very well prepared, are you? Woefully inadequate, as a matter of fact. How do you plan to pull off your fantasy when you supposedly can't remember the details, Mr. Case?"

He didn't answer. He just pressed his lips into a narrow, unforgiving line.

"Well?" she asked, but then the plane jerked to a halt, and everyone began to bustle with their luggage and belongings.

"Saved by the bell," Trevor announced. "We're in Paris."

"But you didn't answer my ques—"

"Listen, everyone," Marie-Ange interrupted. "Welcome to Paris. Everything has been arranged by Framboise to make your stay enjoyable. If you will all follow me . . ."

Annie's attention wandered from Marie-Ange's instructions as she glanced around in surprise. When had they survived the awful, gear-grinding, seat-thumping landing she'd been so afraid of? She hadn't even noticed, and here they were, on the ground. If she didn't know better, she would've been very suspicious that Mr. Case had prodded her into an argument on purpose, just to keep her fevered mind off the landing.

"No," she said firmly, which earned her a curious look from Jamie. Trevor simply wasn't the sort of person who'd start an argument just to soothe a bad case of jangled nerves.

Besides, if she thought that, then she might have to consider thanking him for getting her through the landing without a heart attack, and she really didn't want to do that.

No, the longer she thought about it, the surer she became. Trevor had poked into her fantasy simply because he liked to annoy her, not for any humanitarian reasons. She had no more time to consider the issue, because Marie-Ange cleared her throat and began again.

"Please keep your baggage with you," the woman from Framboise ordered. "Our limousines should be waiting, but we must stay together as a group. We don't want anyone to get lost."

Annie struggled to her feet, swinging herself and her carryon bag out into the aisle. "My first trip to Paris," she whispered.

Here she was, on her maiden voyage to the City of Lights, feeling tipsy and dizzy from too much champagne, a nervous wreck from riding on a plane, an even worse nervous wreck from sitting far too close to Casanova Case.

"I still think he's hiding something," she whispered stubbornly.

Annie frowned. He had to know what he'd entered, didn't he? Her champagne-fogged brain was having trouble coming up with an answer to this paradox, and

Marie-Ange was fussing at them to hurry along, so she deferred that question to another time.

Don't worry, Mr. Case, she promised him silently. *I will find out what this is all about.*

They were herded through the airport and stuffed into a fleet of dove gray limousines, cheek to jowl with Princess Kerenza's sixteen pieces of matched luggage, and three steamer trunks that would've sunk the *Titanic* all by themselves. Thankfully, the others had packed more lightly, and everything did eventually get wedged in, soothing Marie-Ange's anxiety somewhat.

Annie knew she should be exhausted after the long plane ride, not to mention the hefty time change, but she was actually exhilarated. Even the air seemed to smell different and more exciting now that she was in Paris, and the sunset diffused over the charming rooftops of the city looked spectacular to her dazzled eyes.

"That was the Arc de Triomphe!" she exclaimed, craning her neck to see out the smoked glass of the limo.

"Of course it was," Kerenza snapped. "What do you think, you silly goose?"

But Annie ignored her. So far, she loved every minute of Paris, even with the portly princess's snotty interference. Surreptitiously Annie scribbled a few notes in a small notebook, trying to record her observations while they were still fresh. After all, she thought cynically, *Undercover USA* expected to get something out of her trip, and she was going to have to start putting details on paper.

They had left the bustling Champs Elysées and were now slowly motoring through a plush, expensive-looking area, full of imposing embassies, aristocratic salons, and grand mansions. Annie kept taking notes, furiously recording the names off the buildings. Maxim's de Paris, Louis Féraud, Hermès . . . They were names she'd read in glitzy books about rich people.

"The Toad is going to love this," she murmured, even though there wasn't anything particularly newsworthy about it. But still—it was local color, wasn't it?

She wasn't sure where she'd expected to stay, perhaps in a charming garret on the Left Bank, reminiscent of Hemingway or Picasso. Or perhaps in the French version of a Holiday Inn—comfortable and unpretentious, if hardly *Parisien*.

But this . . . Well, all she could say was, "Wow." They were definitely on the Right Bank, definitely on high-toned turf, as the limos pulled up in front of an impressive old building. Could this be the hotel? As Annie stared up at it, she took in the expanse of soft gray stone, mansard-roofed, with a flurry of scrolls and gargoyles ornamenting the windows, and charming black iron grillwork laced across the balconies. The discreet bronze plaque next to the front doors proclaimed it to be the Hotel Séchelles.

Good grief. The place was fabulous! She half expected Princess Grace and a royal entourage to come sweeping out the door. Except for the fact that Princess Grace was dead, of course. Now, that *would* be a story for the readers of *Undercover USA*. *Princess Grace is alive and well and living in splendor at the Hotel Séchelles!*

Annie frowned. Here she was, being treated like a princess, and all she could think of was twisting it into something tabloid readers would find palatable. Smiling grimly, she stuffed her notebook into the pocket of her suit jacket before she changed her mind. There was no way she was going to spoil these moments by recording them for the readers of *Undercover USA*.

"It's lovely," she whispered as she and the others were ushered into the hotel. Inside, the small, marble-floored foyer opened onto a tiny but exquisite salon, filled with delicate Louis XV–style chairs and settees. The others fussed with their bags in the lobby, but

Annie couldn't resist poking into the salon, breathing in the scent of polished antiques and fresh flowers.

"Wow," she said again. For a writer, she was remarkably short of words. But the flowers . . . They were everywhere, piled high in formal arrangements that wouldn't have looked out of place at Versailles. She could no more have sat in that room and felt like she belonged than she could have walked into the White House and demanded dinner. Outside in the lobby, she heard Princess Kerenza's high-pitched voice, spoiling the mood, drawing Annie back to reality.

"But I always stay at the Ritz when I'm in Paris," Kerenza complained. "How will my friends know where to find me?"

As Marie-Ange patiently explained that all of the finalists were required to stay at the Hotel Séchelles for the duration of the contest, Annie burned the portly princess with a glare. The place was spectacular, and she didn't appreciate Kerenza's comments. Besides, she couldn't have cared less if this wasn't the Ritz, or the Taj Mahal, for that matter. She loved it.

As soon as she had her key, she took off up the marble-paneled staircase, eschewing the elevator and the company of her competitors. Marie-Ange called something after her, but Annie kept going, in a hurry to see her own room. She was afraid she would be disappointed, that it would be cramped or shabby or simply boring. But when she arrived on the top floor, huffing and puffing from all the stairs, she saw that her room was every bit as beautiful as the lobby, every bit as light and airy and elegant. It was a whole lot cozier, too, from the window seat to the tall, old-fashioned bed.

The room was decorated in cream and soft yellow, with enameled woodwork and furniture. There was one simple armchair, covered in pale lemon silk, pulled up to a dainty ormolu writing desk, and one painting, a landscape in pastel greens and yellows, hung over the white marble fireplace on the far wall.

A fireplace! Her room had its own fireplace!

And the bathroom! Holy smokes! It was all marble, including a Jacuzzi and gold taps that she couldn't believe were real.

Annie had never bothered much with furnishings or interior decoration. She'd never had time. Her company apartment had come already done up in a rather institutionalized beige decorating scheme, to which she'd added her own garage-sale bookshelves and filing cabinets.

It had never bothered her to live in a place where the mood and the decor had nothing to do with her personality. But now that she'd seen the absolutely perfect surroundings of the Hotel Séchelles, she wasn't sure she'd ever want to leave. She could see herself curled up on that window seat, reading *A Moveable Feast* while a fire crackled in the fireplace. And then slipping in for a hot bath in her Jacuzzi.

"I could get used to this," she said happily.

She couldn't help a feeling of euphoria as she pushed open her French windows and breathed in deeply of the heady evening air. She barely poked her head out onto the balcony, but it was far enough to catch the view of a very pretty little courtyard down there.

Of course her balcony overlooked the courtyard. It was just one more sign that everything was going beautifully, that fate and karma and good luck were on her side. The air was decidedly cool, but Annie left the windows open, enjoying the fresh breeze.

Her luggage hadn't arrived upstairs yet, so she knew it was foolish, but she couldn't resist shrugging out of her stuffy jacket and skirt, and tossing them carelessly on the bed. Then she hopped into the cool marble bathroom to splash some water on her face. She started to hum "April in Paris" but couldn't get past the first few bars, so happily switched to "Isn't It Romantic?" the theme song for the wonderful contest that had landed her in this fabulous place.

It was such a great song, and she was so happy here in Paris, taking the first steps toward what she now felt sure was a bright future with a wonderful job, that she almost didn't notice she was starting to sing it out loud and to dance around the room, waving her arms in time to the song.

"Isn't it romaaaaaaaantic?" she belted out from the foot of her bed. There she was, perched on the bed, wearing nothing but a camisole and half-slip, emoting in the general direction of the fireplace, when she heard a funny noise from over by her balcony.

Was that a cough?

She stilled. There was another one. A polite, throat-clearing cough, as if someone were trying to tell her she wasn't alone.

She stood there for a moment, afraid to contemplate what or who might be there. But in her heart, she already knew. Who else had been haunting her every footstep since the contest had begun? Who else but Trevor?

When she turned, her worst fears were realized. Trevor Case was standing on her balcony, watching her, his narrow, sexy lips twitching with suppressed laughter.

Annie could feel her entire body suffuse in a rosy blush. She wished desperately she were wearing something less revealing and more attractive than her sissy white cotton camisole and half-slip.

"May I come in?" he asked, as he slipped in through the French windows without waiting for her answer.

"Don't you dare come in here," she hollered, snatching her jacket up off the bed, slamming her arms into the sleeves, and buttoning it up tight. "What are you doing here, anyway, you Peeping Tom?"

"Sorry," he said cheerfully. "Our rooms share a balcony."

"You're next door?" Her fantasy of the perfect room went up in smoke. It didn't matter how perfect it was if Trevor Case was only a heartbeat away. "Even if you are next door, that's no excuse for you to come over here and spy on me."

"Sorry," he said again. But he didn't look sorry. Not with that hot spark of mischief in his eyes and that crooked smile on his face. Damn the man. "If it's any consolation," he added, "you looked great in your, uh . . . whatever it was you were wearing. And you do a version of 'Isn't It Romantic?' like nobody else's."

"Thank you," she returned stiffly. Complimenting her on the way she looked in her underwear? And making fun of her singing, too, all in the same breath. The man was insufferable. "Did you come over here for a reason, or just to humiliate me?"

"You have nothing to be ashamed of," he said warmly. His gaze swept over the parts of her that had so recently been uncovered, and she blushed all over again.

"Well, I am, okay? I feel like a goon."

Good grief! Why had she told him that? There was no reason to let him know he'd gotten to her. She might as well concede victory to the maddening jerk right now and get it over with.

Turning away, she wrenched her skirt on, in her haste scrunching the soft cotton of her slip into an uncomfortable bunch around her waist. And then she couldn't get the damn zipper to close on the side because all the extra fabric was in the way. She ignored the indignity, letting the stupid thing sag open. Squaring her shoulders, Annie faced Trevor Case down.

"Are you going to tell me what you're doing here?" she demanded.

"I, uh, have a message," he said distantly. His eyes were glued to her skirt where it gaped open.

"Well?" she prompted. "What's the message?"

He smiled then, giving her the willies. He was enjoying this, every single second of her distress, and it was driving her crazy. What kind of man climbed in someone else's French windows and then acted like he owned the place, perfectly at ease, as if he'd been given an engraved invitation? A man like Trevor Case, obviously.

"Since you left the lobby before everyone else," he said pleasantly, "you didn't hear the instructions. And since I was assigned the room next to yours, Marie-Ange asked me to come over and fill you in."

"So? Get filling, will you?"

"First item on the agenda is tomorrow morning," he told her. He was so smooth and unruffled, he might as well have been a damn tour guide. "We have a press conference at Framboise headquarters, which is practically across the street, but they're sending limos to pick us up anyway. After that, there's a luncheon, and then we head right into Kerenza's fantasy."

"From her essay, you mean?"

"I'd be surprised if she actually wrote one," Trevor said dryly. "But she's doing something for us tomorrow, at any rate. Apparently her fantasy required the least setup, so Marie-Ange made her go first. We'll draw straws tomorrow to see who goes next."

"Hopefully you'll be able to remember your fantasy by the time it's scheduled to go," she said snidely, trying to prod a sensitive area, but he didn't offer any response. After waiting a moment, she prompted, "Is that it? The end of your message?"

"That's it." His smile widened.

"Okay, so you can leave now, right?"

"Uh-huh."

She marched to the door, opening it as far as it would go, revealing the quiet corridor. "Be my guest."

"Just enjoying the view."

"There's nothing to see," she managed between gritted teeth, grabbing the open part of her skirt and holding it together in one hand. "Now, go. Or I'll call Marie-Ange and complain about you again."

"So you admit you did it the first time?"

"You already knew that," she snapped back.

"Yeah, I did." His smile didn't falter as he ducked back out the window and onto the balcony. "See you in the morning, Annie. I can't wait."

"Oh, brother," she muttered, slamming the door with a healthy smack.

What the heck was she going to do about Trevor Case? The man was getting worse and worse, while she was struggling not to be swept away with the tide.

"He's a menace," she said out loud. And then she got busy trying to straighten out the mess her clothing was in. Yet another disaster to lay at the door of the Legal Lothario.

FIVE

Sitting in a posh salon off the Rue du Faubourg-Saint-Honoré, Annie was twiddling her thumbs, biding her time, singing verses of "Ninety-nine Bottles of Beer on the Wall" under her breath.

If things didn't pick up soon, she swore she was going to commit murder. Preferably the murder of Princess Kerenza, the cause of this endless tedium. She stared daggers at Kerenza's curvacious chest, overflowing from some sort of glittery high-fashion evening dress, but it didn't change anything.

"Damn the woman," she whispered darkly, but there was no one within earshot to care that she was bored out of her gourd.

"I'm in Paris," she murmured. Who'd ever have believed it was possible to do anything so deadly dull, so incredibly tiresome, in the most exciting city in the world?

And it had started out to be such a promising day—Annie's first day in Paris, her first glimpse of the Seine in the misty light of morning (if she poked her head out onto her balcony and craned her neck as far as possible, she caught sight of something vaguely gray-blue that she felt sure must be the river), and her first taste of café au lait and croissants on the hotel's leafy little terrace.

As Annie had sat idly on the terrace, sipping her steaming coffee and feeling like a real *Parisienne*, she'd mulled over the possibilities. She had envisioned a leisurely walk down the byways of Paris, perhaps a stop or two at a bookstore or a boulevard café. Maybe she'd wander over to Notre-Dame cathedral, or stroll through the Tuileries gardens. Maybe a nice, kind Frenchman, someone who had absolutely nothing in common with one Trevor Case, would offer to buy her an ice cream cone in the park.

After all, she was in Paris. Anything was possible.

She had a whole pile of guidebooks back in her room, with all sorts of tidbits flagged for future reference, just waiting to be tried and tasted and savored. She knew she had contest duties to attend to, but surely before she had to go act responsible, she'd have time for a few adventures. . . .

Wrong.

Before she knew it, she'd been scooped up and tucked into a limo with the other contestants. Squashed in between Kerenza and Jamie as they drove the few blocks to the Framboise office, Annie had no chance to even catch a glimpse of any landmarks or famous sights.

Worse, the close quarters wreaked havoc with her favorite leopard-print silk crepe suit. With Kerenza practically on top of her, the pleats in Annie's skirt got all wrinkled, and a button was almost pulled off the front of her long, straight jacket. She wrenched it back into shape, casting a malevolent gaze at Kerenza as the woman gabbed on about how many famous people she knew in Paris, flapping her hands in the air and taking up much more than her fair share of the seat.

Annie gritted her teeth and held her temper. After all, it could've been worse. At least Trevor was safely in the front seat, well out of view now that her skirt kept flipping up, exposing most of her thigh. With him to contend with, she truly would've hurled herself out the car door and into the maelstrom of Paris traffic.

Luckily, the uncomfortable ride didn't last long. Framboise Champagne International was housed in a very old, very elegant building, next to an embassy on one side and an exclusive antique store on the other. It was a pretty building, if a bit stodgy, but there was no time to gawk, as they were ushered upstairs and into a large, formally appointed room, bustling with reporters and photographers speaking in a hubbub of French and English.

The four contestants were welcomed by a receiving line of well-dressed men, with the president of Framboise, a very distinguished gentleman named Georges Collot, at the head of the line. Princess Kerenza plugged up the works when she stopped to fawn over Monsieur Collot, but he quickly disengaged her from his arm, turning to Trevor Case instead. As a matter of fact, he seemed very pleased to meet Trevor, and the two men stood chatting there for some time, while Annie and Jamie languished behind them.

Whether this hearty welcome, man to man, was just a ruse to get rid of Kerenza, or whether Monsieur Collot really did find Trevor fascinating, Annie couldn't tell. At any rate, they finally finished their talk, and she continued down the line, shaking hands perfunctorily, all the way down to a sweet young man called Bertrand.

"He is my assistant," Marie-Ange informed her. "Bertrand will be your liaison to my office, to help you with whatever you need to create your fantasies. Isn't that right, Bertrand?"

"Yes, mademoiselle," he offered politely. But his cheeks began to get very pink, and his gaze was focused directly on his shoes.

"I'm sure Bertrand's help will be wonderful," Annie said warmly, trying to pull the poor thing out of his funk, but Bertrand continued to stare at his feet. She had a feeling he wasn't going to be a whole lot of help.

After the introductions were completed, Annie and the others were shepherded around to a podium, where they were formally presented to the media. Marie-Ange did all the talking, even though Princess Kerenza tried to get herself into the limelight several times. But Marie-Ange successfully quelled the interruptions, pulling the press conference along at a steady pace.

Annie had no desire to utter a word, not after noticing a photographer from *Undercover USA* sneaking around the edges of the crowd. She dipped a hand in front of her face, but she knew that was no camouflage.

The photographer was only too easy to spot. His slicked-back hair, thick, droopy mustache, and sleazy grin were unmistakable. Annie recognized him as a particularly odious person named Wendell, who would've wormed his way inside the gates of hell if he'd thought there was a picture there. His favorite assignments involved taking portraits of dead celebrities in their caskets.

Annie began to feel very nervous. What in the world was Wendell doing here? Checking up on her? Or maybe her boss, old C. Todd Entwhistle himself, had sent some sort of message via the grubby photographer. It was too horrifying to contemplate.

She felt like the word "traitor" was stamped on her forehead. Who exactly she was betraying, she hadn't figured out yet; it was a toss-up between the tabloid she worked for and the contest she'd entered under a misleading name. She wasn't technically being on the up-and-up with either, although she wasn't really hurting anyone at this point.

It didn't matter. She still felt guilty.

But she did her best to ignore Wendell's presence,

to pretend that Trevor Case was not standing directly behind her, breathing down her neck, and to act like a normal contestant in the middle of a press conference. Thankfully, no one talked to her much, and Wendell kept his distance across the phalanx of photographers.

As the lights flashed, she tried gamely to smile. She noted, with some amusement, that Trevor Case was no happier than she was to be the center of all this attention. First he up and disappeared for several long moments, and Marie-Ange had to send her little gofer, Bertrand, looking for him.

Even after Case was brought back into the fold, he didn't really cooperate. Sticking his hands in the pockets of his expensive suit jacket, he gave the crowd of reporters a ferocious glare, as if he wished he were anywhere but in front of them.

There they were, bunched together in an awkward lump so that the photographers could snap pictures of the four lucky winners at the same time. Kerenza thrust herself out front and center, of course, beaming all the way, while Jamie and Annie sort of hovered off to one side. Case ducked behind them, almost completely blocked, and he only agreed to move closer after considerable haranguing.

"Smile," Marie-Ange hissed at him, and he managed a sort of stern, thin-lipped grimace that was nothing like the knock-your-socks-off smile he'd blazed at her.

Apparently the Legal Lothario didn't relish the idea of seeing his mug on the front of every paper in France, not to mention America. Or maybe he just didn't want his picture taken with the likes of her and Princess Kerenza hanging on him. Feeling mischievous, Annie leaned over, linking an arm through his and yanking him closer, just as a dozen photographers snapped them.

It was a lame joke at best, and she was immediately

sorry. Case didn't seem to be sorry at all, gazing down at her with a truly evil expression that sent tingles all the way down to her toes. He snuggled even closer, clasping a hard arm securely around her waist, until she could feel the heat and the strength of him branding her through the thin silk of her suit.

"Playing with fire, Annie?" he whispered.

All she could do was lick her lips and stare up into his sexy gray eyes. It wasn't fair for a man to be so gorgeous, so smart, so charming, so *perfect*.

She wanted him to say her name again, in that husky, spine-tingling voice. She wanted him to bend down and press those narrow, mocking lips up against hers. Hard. She wanted him any way she could get him.

But then, with his arm still wrapped around her like that, holding her fast, he turned and flashed a dazzling smile for the cameras. Blinking, she came back to reality. For a moment there, she'd forgotten they weren't alone. But she knew with dreadful certainty what that picture would turn out like. Her dazed, him triumphant . . .

As if they'd been caught in the throes of something very naughty.

"Looks like some of your contestants are really getting into this romance thing," one of the American reporters snickered.

Annie could feel her face suffuse with hot color. Quickly, before she had a chance to change her mind, she trod down hard on Case's foot, until he yelped with pain and had to let her go.

"That'll teach you," she muttered. Somehow, she doubted he took the lesson to heart. But she slipped over to safety, on the other side of Kerenza, where she knew Case wouldn't follow.

Blessedly, the press conference didn't last long, and the *Undercover* photographer, who kept trying to catch her eye, was pushed out the door with the rest of them. Annie had no intention of receiving any messages from her Toad of a boss until she was good and ready. And she certainly didn't want any knowing winks or comradely gestures from that horrid Wendell, just the thing to tip Case and the others off to the connection between her and the tabloid. She shivered just thinking about it.

But her secret was safe as they filed into lunch, set up in a small, private garden behind the Framboise building. As a matter of fact, any secret she had was safe, since she was apparently the only person present who didn't speak French. As she nodded politely, eating whatever was put in front of her, the conversation whirled around her in a meaningless jumble of *biens* and *mercis*.

Annie felt like an absolute ninny as Trevor and Jamie happily conversed with the brass. Kerenza was off and running, hip-deep in a story in which the name Maurice Chevalier appeared prominently. And Trevor—well, he even told a joke that ended in something that sounded like *poulet*, which she thought she remembered from French menus as meaning chicken. A joke about chicken? It didn't sound remotely funny to her. No matter; it had the rest of the table roaring.

No one had suggested that fluency in French was required for this trip, or for the Romance Ambassador job. So why did she already feel at a disadvantage?

After lunch, amid much fanfare, they got ready to draw slips of paper from a glass bowl, to determine in what order they would play out their fantasies. They already knew Kerenza was going first, of course, although she certainly didn't seem to be expending any effort on the project.

"All set?" Marie-Ange asked sharply, to which Kerenza replied, "Were you speaking to me?"

"Are you all set?" the Frenchwoman asked again.

"Oh, I suppose," Kerenza said carelessly, waving a hand laden with heavy rings. "Do you notice how the light catches my diamonds?"

Annie had the urge to let Kerenza know just how little any of them cared about her stupid diamonds, but she refrained. Instead, she drew the first slip from the bowl. Her stomach did a quick flip-flop as she unfolded the paper, but she was relieved to find she had number four.

"Last," she announced with a wide smile. Going last, she'd have plenty of time to make sure everything was perfect for her version of a fantasy evening. Plus she'd be able to see what the others did, to know how her idea matched up. Yes, last was definitely the best position to be in for the contest.

Jamie drew next, and she took third. She also seemed relieved, although she murmured absently that she was going to have to get to work right away, as her fantasy was rather elaborate. Immediately she took Bertrand, the assistant, aside, and began peppering him with questions about costumes and country houses from the seventeenth century. *Heavens*, Annie thought, that *did* sound elaborate.

Since Annie was going to be last, and Jamie had drawn next to last, that left the number-two spot for Trevor. His expression was noncommittal, but there was a hard line to his jaw that convinced Annie he wasn't thrilled to be next in line.

"Need any help?" she asked cheekily, just to see if she'd get a reaction.

"No, thank you," he said in a forbidding tone.

"Just asking." She smiled. "In case your fantasy was elaborate, too, like Jamie's."

"It's not."

"Sure?"

"Sure."

Well, one thing was sure. Trevor Case was not happy with some aspect of his proposed romantic fantasy. Or maybe he was still pretending he didn't remember what it was.

"You could always cancel yours," she told him as

they were herded back out to the limo for the onset of whatever little drama Kerenza had planned. Case took the front seat again, and Annie scooted all the way forward to declare, "You could just drop out. No harm done. Mine's very good, and I'm sure Jamie's is, too, so skipping yours wouldn't be that much of a hardship."

"I'm not canceling."

"Just trying to be helpful."

"Uh-huh," he said dubiously.

It wasn't long before the driver pulled up in front of their destination, the epitome of chic, the Yves Saint-Laurent boutique on Avenue Marceau. It seemed a funny place to begin a romantic fantasy, even for Princess Kerenza, but Annie dutifully smoothed out the wrinkles in her suit, tried to boost her ego enough that she wouldn't feel out of place in such high-toned surroundings, and followed the others inside the small bastion of haute couture.

As the gaggle of people from Framboise were guided toward chairs, Kerenza flashed them all a broad smile. "Please take your seats," she said grandly. "I'll only be a moment. And then you shall all see the most romantic sight in the world—a beautiful woman in a beautiful dress."

It was clear the pudgy princess was counting herself as the beautiful woman in question, although Annie had her doubts it was appropriate. But Kerenza swept off, into a private dressing room somewhere behind the scenes of Yves Saint-Laurent.

"What is she doing?" Annie asked. "Is this part of her fantasy?"

"It appears so," Marie-Ange replied grimly.

There were quite a few grumbles, but the Framboise big shots as well as the contestants shuffled into chairs and waited for the next step. It didn't take long. Before they'd had a chance to figure out escape routes, Kerenza reappeared, positively preening inside a red-and-black-spotted chiffon party dress slashed dangerously low in the front and then puffed out like a tutu below the waist.

"She can't be serious," Annie muttered, in awe at the sheer volume of the dress. "How can she do the rest of her fantasy wearing *that*?"

There was no answer, and no need for one, since Kerenza didn't do anything in that particular outfit. All she did was take a few spins and then dash off to put on another dress, this one a strapless silver beaded thing, complete with a three-foot-tall feathered hat.

"Wait a minute," Trevor said suddenly. "Are you telling me *this* is her fantasy, playing fashion show while we watch?"

Marie-Ange sighed loudly. "It appears so," she said again, casting anxious looks at her boss, Monsieur Collot, who appeared none too pleased.

Annie was confused. "But how did she get to be a finalist with such a stupid idea?"

The woman from Framboise swallowed uncomfortably, taking a long pause before she began. "I'm afraid the princess neglected to write an essay," she said reluctantly, "so we were uncertain exactly what she would present." She lowered her voice. "She was our previous spokesperson, you understand, and it was felt by those in charge that she ought to be included as a finalist, even though she did not technically prepare an entry."

"Terrific." Annie crossed her arms over her jacket. "First Case is in because he's a guy, and now the dopey princess makes it without even having to compete. I'm beginning to have serious doubts about this contest."

"How dare you suggest that I made it because I'm a man!" Trevor demanded. "You have no reason to cast aspersions on my entry."

"Oh, yeah? Tell him, Marie-Ange." Annie waited

for Marie-Ange to clarify matters, but the French-woman kept her lips pressed together in a thin line.

"There is nothing wrong with my contest!" she said finally.

"Shhhh," warned Kerenza, tripping out in front of them in a lime green halter dress decorated with cascading fringe. "You don't want to miss anything."

Annie shielded her eyes from the glow of the violently green gown, still not quite believing that this was all there was to Kerenza's entry in the contest. This fashion-show nonsense was bizarre, hideous, and spectacularly unromantic. Yechhh.

After inflicting five or six more unflattering ensembles on her captive audience, the princess waved a hand at the vendeuse, who scurried to package everything up for this one-in-a-lifetime client. And then Kerenza waltzed out, intent on dragging everybody to the next couturier on her list.

The whole group paraded from Saint-Laurent to Guy Laroche, from Christian Dior to Christian Lacroix. Everywhere they went, Annie saw beautiful things—dresses and scarves, handbags and belts—but all she got to look at was the portly princess, stuffed into one awful outfit after another. Her favorites (on the all-time worst clothes list) were a purple and blue flounced thing that resembled a thunderstorm in progress, and a fuzzy bouclé suit with fur cuffs and collar, which made Kerenza look like a giant poodle.

At this last display of horrifying excess, Annie had trouble keeping her lunch down. Clearly this was no romantic fantasy at all, just an excuse for Princess Kerenza to acquire a new wardrobe at Framboise expense. If only the woman had better taste . . .

Unfortunately, there was no polite way to leave. Annie considered feigning illness, just long enough to get out on the streets, where she could do some sightseeing. But Marie-Ange kept scanning the room with a pained expression on her face, an expression Annie could read only too well. *If I'm stuck here, then so are the rest of you.*

Annie sighed, shuffling in her seat to find a more comfortable position. Her salary at the tabloid had put a terrific wardrobe within reach, and Annie dearly loved nice clothes. As a matter of fact, shopping was her one real vice. She particularly loved this leopard-print suit, with its respectable lines and snappy fabric, but at the moment, she would've gladly traded it for a pair of old jeans and a sweat shirt.

This was torture. She really had to get out of this place, before Kerenza dragged them out of the current boutique and on to yet another fancy store. If she had to look at one more low-cut evening gown plastered on that too large body, Annie knew she couldn't be held responsible for her actions.

Meanwhile, Jamie was behaving like an angel, managing wan smiles each time Kerenza trooped out in another fleshy cocktail dress. The romance novelist had pulled paper and pen out of her purse, and she was rapidly working on something, so perhaps she'd decided to write a new book while held hostage by Kerenza's warped fantasy.

Marie-Ange and her assistant, the young Bertrand, were right up front, ramrod-straight and pretending to pay attention, while the big bosses, including Monsieur Collot, dozed in the back.

Clearly, everyone was bored stiff.

Everyone except Trevor. On Annie's left, he was looking definitely twitchy. With a clenched jaw and a fierce air of concentration, he kept glancing at his watch, jiggling his leg, drawing his dark brows together as he stared into space. Twice Annie intercepted his gaze by accident, although both times she looked away at once.

Chicken, she chided herself. *Poulet* was more like it, now that she was in France. But it was the same problem whichever language she used. She was afraid of him. As if merely looking at the man was going to give her a heart attack. Well, maybe it was.

But there was something about him that kept pulling her eyes back, something more than just the obvious sinful good looks. No, she got the distinct feeling that something funny was up with Trevor Case. She saw him scanning the room, and especially the door, as if he were judging how long it would take him to sneak out. And then he sent this measuring gaze past each of the important Framboise people, just to make sure he knew where they were.

He's planning an escape. Suddenly she knew it was true. Trevor had every intention of staging a breakout.

"If he's going, I'm going with him," Annie vowed under her breath.

Even as she thought it, she caught a glimpse of movement from his direction. Sure enough, quick as lightning, Case was sliding to the end of his row, sneaking for the door.

Without a second thought, Annie went after him.

"Hallelujah," Trevor said out loud, offering a rakish smile to a pretty French girl passing by on the sidewalk.

The "hallelujah" wasn't for her so much as his own new found freedom. It felt great. A brisk spring breeze batted at him, dispelling the rich, perfumed odor of the last salon, and he breathed in deeply, striding rapidly down the sidewalk, eager to put Christian Lacroix and Louis Féraud and all the rest far behind him.

So far today, he'd done absolutely nothing of any utility. He'd wasted his time and cooled his heels, pretending to be a good little contestant. But that pose was over.

Purposefully Trevor made his way down Rue du Faubourg-Saint-Honoré, heading straight back to the Rue Royale, which, as he recalled, was very near the Framboise office. It was several blocks away, but he kept on walking, welcoming the exercise and the freedom after so much idle time cooped up in those hellacious boutiques and salons.

But he had no time for regrets. At the moment, Trevor had only one thing on his mind. It was the same problem he'd been mulling over ever since he'd drawn that damn number in the fantasy lottery.

He was next.

In two or three days, he was expected to pull off a romantic fantasy, fantastic enough to dazzle every schoolgirl in the continental U.S.A., as well as a few French businessmen and one little cynic named Annie Jonesborough. His pride was on the line here. Unfortunately, he had no idea what he was supposed to do.

Or, more precisely, he had no idea what lame-brained idea his precocious little nieces had concocted for him when they'd entered him in the "Isn't It Romantic?" contest. He'd tried calling them last night to find out, but their mother said they were off to some fancy arts camp in upstate New York, at a location purposely without telephones.

He was stumped. And he had no clue what they'd written. With Zoë and Veronica at the helm, anything was possible. Although he felt sure he wasn't going to like enacting whatever it was they'd written, he could only hope it wasn't too disgusting.

What could they have done? As far as he knew, the girls' idea of erotic was a long-haired rock star wedged into leather pants.

"Good lord," he muttered, momentarily stopped in his tracks. "Anything but that."

Well, there was no point in worrying about it. Not until he knew for sure what Zoë and Veronica's fantasy was. And the only way to find out was to storm the Framboise office, preferably now, while everyone was occupied with Kerenza's fashion fiasco. Once inside, he would either sweet-talk some nubile secretary, or go the cat burglar route and break in, if he had to.

One way or another, he was determined to find Marie-Ange's files, and steal a copy of his nieces' entry.

Of course, he could've just canceled his fantasy and dropped out of the contest, as Annie had suggested. He smiled just thinking of his wily little adversary. Today she'd looked good enough to eat. And he'd been sorely tempted when she'd sidled up next to him during the photo session.

His smile widened. She wouldn't try that kind of stunt again any time soon, if he was any judge.

But still . . . Trevor shook his head. What was he going to do with her? There she was today, with her blond hair in that snippy little bob, and her wide blue eyes as innocent as a china doll's. She wore her skirts short enough to cast any thought of innocence right out of his head, however. She had terrific legs, and there was a lot of them showing under that flippy skirt she'd worn today. Short, pleated, and in a fabric that looked like some exotic brand of jungle cat. He had the urge to growl just thinking about it.

He'd like to get his hands on that skirt, and on the slippery, crafty competitor inside it. At the moment, however, he had no intention of letting his brains melt enough to touch her.

Maybe all the erotic waves that kept washing over him were part of her plan to beat him in the contest. Or maybe he was being paranoid.

Whatever the answer, she was his adversary, and he took that kind of competition seriously. Even if it meant creating some bizarre teenage rock-star fantasy. He winced, hoping it wouldn't come to that.

But just because Annie would like nothing better than for him to fold, to give up and give in, he wasn't going to do it. If she thought she'd soon be crowing to the world that she'd beaten him, she had another think coming.

"No way, Annie," he said smugly. "It's not over yet."

Hands in his pockets, head high, Trevor kept on walking, headed straight for the Framboise office, for a rendezvous with his very own fantasy.

SIX

Annie was having a very difficult time keeping up. For one thing, his legs were a whole lot longer than hers, and she was practically race-walking just to keep him in sight. For another, he'd had a head start.

Hurrying along behind him, she had to ignore a beautiful little bookstore, and then, even more tempting, a dessert shop where the smell of chocolate hung heavy in the air. Annie cast more than one longing look at the spectacular cakes and truffles piled high in the window.

But still, she was out of the high-fashion torture session Kerenza had devised. That was worth a celebration all by itself, even if she did have to follow Trevor, and pay no attention to the wonderful sights all around her. Annie smiled as she carefully sidestepped a lady who was trying in vain to control three yippy poodles on fancy leather leashes.

"Oh, my goodness," Annie murmured, looking down at the dogs for the first time. "Those poodles are wearing dresses."

But she had no time to gawk at cutesy canines, not if she wanted to continue her pursuit of the elusive Mr. Case. The back of his beautiful dark head was still visible above the crowd, gliding along about half a block ahead of her. What was he doing? More important, where was he headed on this mad dash down the streets of Paris?

They swept past the Elysées Palace, and then the American Embassy, where, as she remembered from one of the guidebooks sitting back in her hotel room, Charles Lindbergh had slept. If she turned and went just a few blocks to the side, she knew she'd bump right into the Place de la Concorde, which was positively stuffed with history. To pass it all by was incredibly frustrating. And for what purpose?

If she shadowed him all this time, and he ended up at an assignation with some long-legged model, she swore she'd kill herself. Or maybe him. Or maybe just the model.

Here, on one of the most fashionable streets in the world, surrounded by beautiful women trailing long scarves and expensive perfume, Annie knew that Trevor must feel right at home. Like the rest of them, he exuded elegance and assurance, wealth and privilege. Damn the man, anyway.

As she squeezed between a couple of well-dressed men puffing on black cigarettes, Annie tortured herself with the idea that Trevor was racing along to meet some blushing beauty. What sort of woman would he choose for a romantic rendezvous on the streets of Paris?

Absolutely spectacular, without a doubt. In a scene right out of a commercial, he would suddenly sweep this fabulous, exotic creature into his arms. Trevor's mystery lady would be wearing dark sunglasses and stiletto heels, with very little in between, as she tossed her fabulous flowing locks and flashed her million-dollar cover-girl smile. All the tourists (and tabloids) would stop to snap pictures of this perfectly matched couple, all long, lean angles and athletic grace, wrapped around each other like two strands of beads on the same necklace.

Boy, that was a depressing thought.

"Why am I following him, anyway?" she asked herself, not for the first time.

It wasn't as if she had a good reason. She could tell herself it had to do with the contest, that she was sure he'd sneaked out to gain some advantage over the other contestants. So, of course, she had to tail him to see what he was plotting.

Unfortunately, she had no real evidence that he was plotting anything.

After all, he could just be out for a walk. Better than anyone, Annie knew how stuffy and stultifying the boutique crawl had become, so she could understand a simple desire to flee. He didn't need any underlying motives for a perfectly logical escape.

But something inside her, some vestige of a reporter's instinct, kept telling her that Trevor Case was up to something, and if she knew what was good for her, she'd follow along and find out what it was.

"He knows as well as I do that Marie-Ange is going to have a hissy fit that we ducked out," Annie mused. "Would he risk getting Marie-Ange all cranky, just for some fresh air? Or would he need a very good reason to take that kind of chance?"

Or was all this speculation just a smoke screen?

"Face it, Annie, you're just hot for the guy," she muttered, glancing ahead to make sure she still had a bead on him. "You've gotten yourself so wrought up with curiosity, you'd follow him right into the river if you had to, just so you could see what he looked like in wet clothes."

Well, she hadn't needed that little bit of self-analysis, had she? For once, she wished she weren't such an honest person.

"This isn't good," she whispered. "Not good at all." It just wasn't healthy to be so preoccupied with Trevor Case. Besides, it was an awkward and irritating thing to have to deal with. For one thing, what was she going to do when she finally caught him?

"It doesn't make any difference," she said abruptly, earning some strange looks from the passersby who heard her talking to herself. But she was still caught up in her pep talk, and she paid no attention.

"Why should my motives matter?" Annie asked herself. Trevor was still behaving suspiciously, and she still firmly believed that by shadowing him, she could find out what was going on. Although she was still deathly afraid he'd end up in the arms of some bimbo at the end of this interminable trek.

Finally she saw the top of his head and the sleeve of his jacket taking a sharp turn off St. Honoré and disappearing down a side street. Heart pounding, she scurried to keep him in sight, squashing past pedestrians, crossing in the middle of the block, taking her life in her hands as cars screeched and honked around her. Annie raced on, paying no attention, rounding the same corner he had, surveying the crowd for a glimpse of her elegant quarry.

"Hellfire!" she said out loud. Where was he? Had she lost him?

No. Annie sighed with relief, sagging against a handy lamppost. There he was, on the opposite side of the street, edging through a gaggle of people around a fancy antique store. He stopped, pretending to gaze into the window, heaped high with an Aladdin's treasure trove of brass candlesticks and porcelain boxes.

"Wait a minute," Annie murmured. "I know that store. It's right next to . . ."

Her gaze swept down the street, as she tried to locate the embassy and the other square stone building she remembered. Yes, there they were. And she knew where she was.

"Framboise," she said softly. "He's prowling around Framboise headquarters."

But why? Had he accidentally left his wallet there? Started a flirtation with one of the secretaries? Or maybe he wanted a quiet tête-à-tête with one of the Framboise bigwigs?

But wait. There was no possibility of a tête-à-tête with anybody, not with most of the company back at the boutique with Princess Kerenza. From Bertrand, the errand boy, all the way up to Monsieur Collot, the president, the Framboise crew were securely occupied elsewhere.

"Everybody's gone," she mused. "Yet he sneaks back here. Why would he come back to an empty building?"

And then it hit her. Maybe precisely *because* it was empty. With everyone else accounted for, Trevor could have the place to himself. He could poke around, pilfer the files . . .

From across the street, Annie narrowed her eyes. Suddenly she knew what Trevor was doing. "His essay," she said out loud. "He doesn't know what's in his essay, and he's going to steal it back."

She hadn't really believed him when he told her he'd forgotten the contents of his essay, but it now appeared to be the truth. Could the man really have no recollection of what he'd written to get into the contest? Back on the plane, the idea had seemed impossible. Now it was the only reasonable explanation.

Annie shook her head. "He's going to break in there, like a bull in a china shop, to steal his own essay." She cast a jaded eye at his progress as he paced in front of the Framboise building. "So what does he do? He cases the joint, in broad daylight, attracting all kinds of attention. He couldn't look more suspicious if he tried."

If she were inclined to help him, which she wasn't, she could've offered a few pointers. As a reporter for a less than respectable newspaper, Annie had learned the hard way how to get into places where she wasn't wanted, and then how to get back out again with a minimum of fuss.

In her life as a tabloid hack, she'd pretended to be a maid, a health inspector, a celebrity dog groomer, an office temp, and even an official government records clerk when it suited her purposes. She'd dug up salient information on movie stars and politicians and business moguls, from places a lot trickier than the half-empty Framboise office.

"I could be in and out of there with his essay in five minutes flat," Annie said with conviction.

As she watched, Trevor set his jaw, swung open the wrought-iron gate, and started to stride up the stone steps toward the front door. He was going to storm the citadel. And ruin everything.

Without a second thought, Annie made up her mind. Jaywalking for the second time that day, she dashed through the traffic. She made it to the other side by the skin of her teeth, while a taxi driver cursed her and a tiny Fiat screeched to a stop behind her. Intent on one goal only, Annie ignored her brush with death in the middle of the boulevard.

"Trevor!" she called out. "Stop!"

He had his hand on the door, but he paused when he heard his name. His dark head swung around, and Annie could tell from the wary expression in his steel gray eyes that he already knew who was waiting.

"I don't believe this," he muttered as she sped up the steps to greet him. "What the hell are you doing here?"

"Saving you from a lot of trouble," she returned briskly.

He raised an eyebrow. "Am I supposed to know what that means?"

"You can't just barge in there and steal it!" Annie fumed. "You have to have a plan."

"Steal what?"

His tone was innocent, but she wasn't fooled. "Your essay, of course. I know why you're here. You sneaked back here to steal your essay from Marie-Ange's files."

There was a pause. "Why would I do a thing like that?" he asked slowly.

"Because you can't remember what's in it," she shot back, impatient with all this dillydallying around the truth. He began to respond, but Annie cut him off quickly. "Don't bother to argue. I already know what you're going to say, and believe me, it doesn't make sense to me, either."

"What?" he demanded.

"You." As a delivery boy gave them a curious glance, Annie pulled Trevor over to one side of the steps and lowered her voice. "You can't expect this to make sense. I mean, really! How could a grown man, one who's supposed to be so darn smart, forget one teensy little essay? Especially since I assume you had to spend some time thinking about it, editing it, making it good, when you wrote it in the first place." Annie frowned. "Although I admit I have difficulty imagining you sitting at your block-long mahogany desk and pondering life's romantic little situations."

Trevor rewarded her with a black scowl, and she knew, with a sudden burst of inspiration, that she'd hit pay dirt.

"Don't tell me," she gasped. "You didn't write it!"

"Be quiet," he hissed.

"Trevor, are you serious? What did you do, toss the entry form at your secretary and tell her to write it?"

"Of course not."

"So how did you . . . ? What did you . . . ?" Annie shook her head. This was a scoop and a half! All she had to do was send one little telegram to C. Toad Entwhistle, and this hotshot competitor, this thorn in her side, was no more. Could she do that? How could she resist?

But already a little voice inside her was crying foul. After all, they were talking about possibly ruining Trevor's life here, perhaps taking away his livelihood. She had more ethical fiber than to wreck a brilliant lawyer's career on something as sketchy as a lame-brained theory that he'd cheated on a contest.

You know you wouldn't do that, Annie. You couldn't. You're not that kind of low-down, mean-spirited troublemaker, and you know it.

"I don't know where you came up with that crazy idea," Trevor said angrily, staring her right in the eye. "But it's patently absurd. Nonsensical. Who in the world would believe that *I* would hire a ghostwriter of some sort, all to enter a goofball contest I couldn't care less about? I think you've lost your mind."

"Hmmm," she speculated, trying to figure out if he was telling the truth. Was it absurd? It sounded like it when he twisted things around in that arrogant way of his, but still . . .

She thought she was on to something. But she didn't have a shred of proof, did she? He certainly wasn't going to admit it, and what he'd said was true enough. No one would believe it.

"And remember, if you tell anyone this fairy tale, I won't take it kindly. I can promise you, Annie, I am a very good attorney, and I have quite a few resources at my command," he said coldly. "I might be inclined to take action to protect my reputation."

She hated it when lawyers threw their weight around. If she'd been sure she wasn't going to rat on him, she almost changed her mind after he tossed out his lawyerly threats. "I've been in court before," she said heatedly. "I can take it."

His gaze got less frosty, more curious. "Why were you in court?"

"None of your business! Besides, if you sued me, all you'd get out of me is about thirty cents."

If he knew who she worked for, however, a lawsuit like that could get him a very decent piece of change. With *Undercover USA* on the other side of the courtroom, Trevor could really go to town seizing corporate assets and asking for injunctions. Talk about socko publicity!

Hardly anyone ever sued the rag for libel, but it had been happening with more frequency of late. And C. Toad was very leery of that kind of thing. If you had proof, even some flimsy statement from a friend of a friend of a friend, it was okay to go with an obviously fake story.

But without so much as a scrap of evidence . . . well, there was no way Annie was going to risk it, even if she were inclined to try. Which she most definitely was not.

"I don't plan on telling anybody," she muttered. "But I still think I'm right."

"Fine, fine," he said hurriedly. "Look, I'm kind of busy. If you take a left here and walk about three blocks, you'll run right into our hotel." He turned to go into Framboise. "I'll see you back there later."

"And what makes you think, for one second, that I would let you up and *dismiss* me, like some school-girl?" Annie demanded. "You need me to pull off this burglary scheme, and I'm stuck to you like glue, buster."

"Oh, Lord," Trevor groaned. "Why me?"

"You need my help," she repeated.

"No, I don't."

"But you admit you came here to rip off your file?"

"No, I do not. I'm not admitting anything." Trevor leaned over, skewering her with his steely gaze. "But I am in a hurry. If you would just leave, I could get on with . . . what I have to do."

"Which is?"

"None of your business."

"You don't seem to understand, Case," Annie said meaningfully. "I've made it my business. I'm coming along whether you like it or not. So you might just as well let me help, because otherwise you're going to have a very noisy, very annoying companion along as you make your little foray into the Framboise fortress. With the attention I'm going to generate, you won't be able to lift anything, including your own wallet."

His eyes narrowed. "You're bound and determined to make my life miserable, aren't you?"

She felt like strangling him. "I'm trying to help you, you moron!"

"Why?" He gave her another one of those searching glances, the ones where his eyes got all smoky and soft. Brother, did she hate it when he did that. "Why would you want to help me?"

"Because you're so obviously making a hash of things." She shrugged. "Let me simply say that, even though you're a lawyer, you're not devious enough for this job."

"I'd stake my deviousness against anybody's," he said slyly.

She didn't like the sound of that at all. "Yeah, well, this is something different. And you're too noticeable, anyway. I mean, who could overlook you?"

"Why, Annie," he said, with a sudden and striking smile, "I think that was a compliment."

"Don't let it throw you." She grabbed his arm and steered him back toward the front door. "Look, we need a plan. Do you, by any chance, know which office it is you want to break into?"

A long pause hung between them, and Annie knew he was considering whether to trust her.

"You don't have a choice," she reminded him.

Finally he said, "Marie-Ange's office. I think our files should be in her office."

"Great. Let's get to it."

Trevor's expression was guarded as he held open the door, and Annie slipped inside the big stone building. As before, they were in a cavernous entrance hall, empty except for a pair of ornate brass elevators along the wall. As she'd expected, Framboise looked practically deserted. Everybody who was anybody was at the salon with Kerenza, and everybody else was taking the opportunity to goof off. Quickly Annie scanned the walls for some kind of directory, to tell them what floor to go to, but there was no handy guide like that around.

"Would you happen to know where we go?" she inquired.

"Fourth floor," he told her, pushing the button for the elevator. "Her office is just around the corner from the room we were in for the press conference. I took a powder while everybody else was busy, and scoped the place out. I saw an office with Marie-Ange's name on the door, and a whole lot of filing cabinets inside. Looked good to me."

"Is there a secretary outside the office?" she asked, probing for possible hazards.

He dismissed it with a shrug. "Down the hall."

"Can you see Marie-Ange's office door from where she sits?"

"Yes, probably." Trevor frowned at her. "Why?"

But Annie ignored the question. "How old was this secretary you saw?"

"Young," he said, in a completely mystified voice. "Maybe twenty, twenty-one. Does that matter?"

"It does if she sits between the elevator and Marie-Ange's office." Annie waited, but he didn't provide her with an answer. "Well?" she prompted. "Does she sit between us and the office?"

"Yes. As a matter of fact, her desk is right outside the elevator. Why?"

Annie sighed. "Because she'll see us get off the elevator, of course, and then watch us waltz right into Marie-Ange's office. What did you think we were going to do, say, 'Hi, how are you, we're planning to rob your boss's office'?"

"If I were by myself," he said testily, "I could probably talk her into letting me into the office. I'd just say Marie-Ange sent me back for something. Her purse, or her itinerary, or something. I don't think it would be too hard."

"I told you, you weren't devious enough." Annie shook her head at the folly of egotistical men. "So you dance in there, and tomorrow she says to Marie-Ange, 'Oh, by the way, that gorgeous Case guy dropped by to get your purse. What a nice guy to come and get it for you.' And Marie-Ange would scream bloody murder, and your goose would be cooked. End of story."

"And what exactly do you propose instead?" he asked sharply. "Scaling the outside of the building, perhaps? A little cat burglary?"

"Well, one thing is for sure," she murmured slowly. She was too absorbed in making a plan to pay any attention to his surly attitude. "We have to get in there, get the goods, and get out, without anybody knowing we were ever there in the first place."

The elevator doors slid open, and Annie started to go in. "Look, here's what we'll do," she told him. "I'll get off a floor before you, and try to find some stairs. You go ahead and get off on the fourth floor, just like you came by specifically to talk to the nubile young secretary. And then you keep her occupied and looking the other direction while I go into the office." She flashed him a sarcastic look. "That shouldn't be too tough for Casanova Case."

"No way." He held the elevator door open, refusing to go in. "I'm stealing my own file. *You* keep the secretary occupied."

"What sense does that make?" Annie protested. "You're the one with all the charm. You're the one with the drop-dead good looks. How likely is it that I could distract her for more than two seconds? Believe me, if she's a run-of-the-mill twenty-year-old female, her radar will pick you up at fifty paces. Even if I stand there breathing down her neck, completely blocking her view, she'll *sense* you're there, and without a qualm, knock me out of the way to get to you. Besides, I don't speak French. What am I supposed to say to her?''

Trevor looked oddly pleased. Serenely he gave up his grip on the elevator door, consenting to come inside next to her. With a smile, he pushed the buttons for the third and fourth floors.

"So you're going along with my plan?" she asked, suspicious of the sudden change in his mood.

"Uh-huh."

"Why?"

He just grinned at her. "Charm, drop-dead good looks, some kind of magnetism that catches unwary young girls at fifty paces . . . Annie, I'm starting to like the way you think."

"You're insufferable," she started, but the doors slid open on her floor, and she had to leave him. "As soon as I have your essay, I'll go back down the stairs and then come back up on the elevator to get you. That way you'll know when it's safe to leave, okay?"

He nodded, already hammering on the button to close the elevator doors.

"Oh, and don't lay it on too thick," she called out to him, but he was already on his way up to his rendez-vous with the poor little secretary. "That girl's not going to know what hit her," Annie muttered.

But meanwhile she had to find some stairs, preferably nowhere near the elevator. She passed various offices, all quiet and unremarkable. There were certainly people working inside—she could hear typewriters and tele-phones occasionally—but nobody ventured out to see what she was doing.

At the end of an L-shaped corridor, she found a door marked SORTIE. "I think that's 'Exit,' " she mur-mured. And indeed, the old wooden door opened with a creak, onto a flight of stairs, going both up and down.

Annie began to feel very nervous about this. It was one thing to put on a good show of bravado for Trevor, but quite another to actually carry out a burglary. "Oh, hush," she said out loud as she crept up the stairs. "What can they do to me even if they catch me?"

The idea of "jail" had a certain ominous ring to it. But Annie kept going, opening the door cautiously onto the fourth floor and peering out into the hallway, a replica of the one down below. Nobody there. Quickly she eased out into the corridor, past several doors, until she was opposite the conference room where they'd met the press earlier that morning, only inches away from the elbow part of the hall. If she rounded the corner, she'd be at Marie-Ange's door, as well as able to see the elevator and the secretary at the end of the hall.

If Trevor and the girl were chatting down there, they were doing it quietly. Annie couldn't hear a thing. Or maybe it was just a very soundproof building. Very carefully she edged around the wall, just far enough to see.

Holy smokes! She shot back around the corner into safety. Trevor and the girl were down there, all right, giggling and parked dead center at the end of the hallway, with a clear view of every speck of dust between here and there. Trevor was so far over the bimbo's desk, he was practically sitting in her lap, but it still didn't obstruct anything.

Damn Trevor Case. What kind of noodlehead was he, to let her think she'd be able to sneak in while he distracted the secretary? There was no way. As soon as she went for the door, the girl would see her. A tank parked in the hallway wouldn't have blocked that view.

"Now for plan B," she whispered. If only she had one. And just as she was really starting to get desperate, she heard the telltale sound of a door opening behind her. She had to hide somewhere fast. But where?

She didn't give herself time to think; she took the first opportunity that fate provided. With a flash of inspiration, Annie went for the door of the corner conference room. Swiftly she bolted inside, hoping against hope that she'd get lucky, and the room would be unoccupied. Safely inside, she stood there with her back to the door, staring into the empty room she'd seen earlier that morning, sending up prayers of thanksgiving.

But it was too soon to celebrate just yet. She might be safe for the moment, but she still had to find a way into Marie-Ange's office and retrieve Trevor's mysterious file.

"How am I going to get inside that office?" she asked out loud. A possibility popped into her head immediately, but she didn't like it one bit.

With a feeling of dread, she walked slowly over to one of the conference room's tall windows, this one facing the same side of the building as Marie-Ange's office. Taking a deep breath, Annie looked outside.

A balcony. She was afraid of that. Every building in France seemed to be teeming with these little wrought-iron balconies. Annie opened the window as quietly as she could manage, poking out her head and spying the length of the balcony.

"Hellfire," she said with disgust. "It goes into Marie-Ange's office."

And since she'd figured out a way to get into that damn office without being seen, she now felt obligated to use it.

Even if it did mean climbing out on a tiny little balcony, risking life and limb for the likes of the Legal Lothario.

"Here goes," she said. And she stuck her leg out the window.

SEVEN

Trevor was losing his cool. After fifteen minutes of idle chitchat with the ditzy young secretary, he had definitely reached his limit. She was a sweet girl, but she wasn't exactly bright, and he had long since run out of conversational topics.

He'd even found himself in the bizarre position of pretending to be pals with Tom Cruise, since she'd plagued him with questions about the movie star since the moment he walked up. Why did she assume he knew Tom Cruise? He had no idea. But it was easier to lie than to think up something else to talk about.

Meanwhile, he still hadn't seen hide nor hair of Annie, or caught any hint of activity near Marie-Ange's door. What the hell was taking so long? If he had to remove this vapid child's hands from his clothing one more time, he was going to explode.

Was it possible that Annie had already made it in and out of the office? He didn't see how. Plus she hadn't appeared yet, although for the last ten minutes, he'd been expecting her to come popping out of the elevator, wearing a triumphant smile and waving his paperwork.

He'd been an idiot to let Annie stick her nose into

his business, especially since he didn't have a clue what her reaction would be once she set eyes on the contest entry his nieces had concocted. How obvious was it going to be that it had been written by a couple of prepubescent girls? Exactly how much trouble was he going to be in?

"Idiot," he swore at himself. But it was too late now.

"*Pardon?*" his pretty young companion asked with a giggle, as if he'd just said something terribly witty.

"Nothing," he told her, manufacturing a wide smile. For the first time in his life, he was acting like he really *was* the Legal Lothario. Too bad, he told himself severely. His conduct might be highly unethical, but he was in too deep to stop now.

But where was Annie? Quickly he made up his mind. He wasn't waiting another minute. He was going into that office himself, no matter where Annie was.

But first he supposed he'd better create some kind of ruse to get Mademoiselle Secretary away from her desk. But what? If he could've maneuvered in English, he would've felt a lot more sure of his chances. In French, lying and scheming were a bit dicier.

"*Chérie,*" he began, rapidly planning ahead so he could manage this in French. He'd thought up the most god-awful story, but it was the best he could do on short notice. "I just realized how perfect you are."

"*Parfait?*" she echoed. "*Pourquoi?*"

"For my friend, Tom Cruise."

"*Ah, oui . . .*" she breathed. "Tom."

"*Oui*, Tom. He's filming his new movie in Paris this week. He told me he needs a beautiful young woman for one special scene, and he asked me if I knew anyone who would fit the bill. At the time," Trevor said, bluffing his best, "I had no one. But now, well, you're perfect. Tom will be thrilled I found you."

"*Moi?*" Her jaw dropped. "*Dans un film avec* Tom Cruise?"

"Bien sûr," he assured her. "You go ahead, and I'll call Tom to let him know you're coming."

With a cry, she leapt to her feet and snatched up her purse. *"Où?"* she demanded. She reached over and grabbed his lapels. *"Où est* Tom Cruise?"

"He's at the Intercontinental Hotel. Right now."

As Trevor watched, the girl dashed off without a second thought. Presumably she was headed for the Intercontinental Hotel, where they would tell her they hadn't seen hide nor hair of Tom Cruise. What a rotten thing to do. But there was no time to wallow in guilt.

As soon as the girl was safely out of range, Trevor took off down the hall, to Marie-Ange's office. The door was unlocked, and he walked right in.

And there she was. Annie. As big as life.

He glowered at her. Next to a tall filing cabinet with one drawer pulled all the way open, she was parked at Marie-Ange's desk, calmly perusing the contents of a slender manila folder. The Trevor Case contest file, no doubt.

"What do you think you're doing?" he demanded. "I've been waiting forever, trying to keep that little dimwit occupied, while you sit down here and cool your heels."

"Oh, pipe down," she said crossly. "I got the file, didn't I? I just didn't have a chance to escape."

"Why couldn't you go back out the way you came in?"

"For your information," she snapped, rising from the desk and shoving the papers back into the file, "I had to come in through the window."

"The window?" Trevor sent a glance in that direction. They were five stories up! "You can't be serious."

Annie glared at him. "Only too serious. There was no way to get down the hall without being seen, so I had to dangle off a rickety little balcony, high over Paris, in high heels, no less."

With the file folder still firmly clasped in one hand, she reached down and grabbed off one of her shoes, brandishing it in the air in her other hand. Considering the evil glint in her eye, he thought it was very likely she intended to strike him with it.

"I broke a heel," she said menacingly. "I ran my stockings. I am very, very cranky. And the only good thing to come out of it was that I got to sit down for a few minutes and read your damn essay." She advanced on him, but her gait was wobbly and uneven now that she was wearing only one of her pumps. "So don't you *dare* yell at me for not getting back to you fast enough!"

Trevor tried hard to suppress a smile. Five-foot-nothing Annie, threatening him with a shoe, clomping up and down while she walked, was a pretty amusing sight. Gently he reached over and removed the heel-less shoe from her grasp. "You might want to take off the other one, too, unless you enjoy masquerading as the Leaning Tower of Pisa."

"You laugh at me, and you're a dead man," she promised.

"Who said I was laughing?"

"Don't even think about it," she shot back. "You owe me, buster. Big time. Because I found your essay." She held up the file folder, right in front of his nose. "If you're nice to me, I might even let you read it."

Trevor smiled. Annie was playing games, but she didn't know yet she was out of her league. "How nice?" he asked softly, leaning in over her, negligently sliding his arms around her waist to pull her nearer, rubbing her shoe against the round curve of her bottom. "This nice, Annie?"

A pretty pink flush crept over her cheeks. "That's, um, a little too nice," she whispered. She tried to pull away, but he held her fast.

He was enjoying her discomfort, enjoying the warm,

wiggly feel of her in his arms, enjoying the way her breath seemed to get caught in her throat. "So," he said, lowering his lips to the curve of her neck, watching her eyes widen and her blush deepen as he pressed a tiny kiss into her soft skin. He could get used to kissing Annie. Unfortunately, there was no time for fun and games at the moment. He murmured, "Are you going to give me my file?"

"It's stuck," she managed. "Stuck between, um, you and me."

"So it is." Regretfully Trevor released her, plucking the folder easily from her limp fingers, setting down her shoe as he flipped open the cover. "And here's my essay, right on top."

Backing up to the relative safety of Marie-Ange's desk, Annie murmured, "I can't wait for you to read it."

Trevor scanned the lines quickly, feeling an immense sense of relief as he finished it up. The girls might be holy terrors, and their writing style might leave something to be desired, but they hadn't painted him into any truly horrifying corners. No, the fantasy evening they'd chosen for him would be a piece of cake, as a matter of fact. Not only was it possible, it was real. He'd done it before.

"So your fantasy takes place in the south of France," Annie remarked dryly. "A yacht, dinner, champagne . . . Not all that exciting."

"It can be," he told her, with a glimmer of mischief. "The right woman, a glass of wine, a little moonlight . . . If it were you and me, Annie, I think it could prove very exciting."

"Uh-huh." She was blushing again. "And why exactly didn't you remember what it was before now? Don't tell me—you've had amnesia since you wrote it."

He shrugged. "It's been a long time."

There was a definite spark of sarcasm in Annie's

voice when she commented, "I'll say it's been a long time. Like maybe fifteen years? That's how long I'd guess it's been since you used words like 'stupendous' and 'awesome.' Let's see, how did it start again? 'My most stupendous idea for a date is to fly a really awesome babe from New York to Saint-Tropez just for dinner.' Awesome babe, huh? You know, Mr. Case, you really have a way with words."

He figured the best thing he could do at this point was keep his mouth shut.

"You no more wrote that than I did," she argued. "Only a bunch of people to whom English is a second language wouldn't have realized immediately that it couldn't have come from you."

Admit nothing, deny nothing, he told himself, much as he would've advised a client. "I'm wounded that you don't like my essay," he said calmly, sticking it back in the file and then replacing the whole thing in the open drawer in the contest section. "Does that mean you don't want to come along when I stage it?"

"What do you mean, come along?"

He turned, in time to see the speculative gleam in her eye. It was foolhardy, but he couldn't resist. "You could be my awesome babe, Annie. You're my first choice."

"I really ought to come along," she muttered. "Just to bother you."

"It's a deal. But first we have to get out of here. We've already wasted too much time." He grinned. "I say we forgo the balcony this time. What do you think?"

"But we can't go out the other way. What about the bimbo?"

He pretended to be insulted. "She's hardly a bimbo. We had a terrific little chat, I'll have you know."

"And I suppose you have a rendezvous scheduled for later, too." Annie shook her head. "Men."

"Once again, you wound me," he told her as he

strode over to the door. "After all, who did I ask along on my romantic fantasy, her or you?"

She began to frame a retort, but he put a finger to his lips as he eased the door open just a crack.

"Come on," he whispered. "And make it quick. Looks like she's still busy with Tom Cruise."

"Tom Cruise? What are you talking about?" Annie demanded, but she let herself be hauled along in her stocking feet, out the door and into the hall.

"Where are the stairs?"

"This way." She led the way back to the stairwell, but stopped abruptly when they reached the exit door. "No, I can't," she said suddenly. "Not without my shoes. Those stairs are filthy, and then on the street . . . Yechh."

"You know, Annie, you're more trouble than you're worth," he said darkly. And then, before she could protest, he swung her up into his arms and started down the stairs, making good their escape from the Framboise Building.

Still in the same clothes, Annie was lying on the bed in her palatial hotel room, with a cool cloth draped across her forehead. She couldn't believe she'd let Trevor Case carry her for a whole block, before he'd found a cab to take them back to the Hotel Séchelles.

"The man is very good at what he does," she mumbled. "I'll give him that."

Too good. Sweeping down the streets of Paris, holding her securely in the circle of his hard, strong arms, he hadn't missed a step, playing Knight in Shining Armor to the hilt. And she hadn't uttered so much as a whimper of protest, either.

"I have no shame," she told herself as she sat up.

So here she was, hiding out in her hotel room, afraid to face him now that he knew how easy she was to mesmerize into submission. "I should've socked him or something," she muttered. "But no. I had to hang on to him like some goofy damsel in distress, gazing up into those beautiful eyes of his like I loved every minute of being hauled down the Rue d'Anglais.''

And then it hit her. ''Good grief,'' she moaned. ''I *did* love every minute of being hauled down the Rue d'Anglais.''

But she didn't have long to stew over it. Before she had time to gather her thoughts, there was a loud pounding on her door.

Her first impulse was to glance at the French windows, to make sure it wasn't Trevor on the balcony again. But no, he would've just walked right in. Besides, this sound was clearly coming from the door.

''Who is it?'' she asked cautiously.

''A message from the U.S.A. for Mademoiselle Porter,'' a rough voice on the other side called back.

It wasn't until she'd taken off the chain and pulled open the door an inch or two that she realized. Nobody in Paris knew that her last name was Porter. She was Anna Jonesborough for the duration of the contest.

Quickly she tried to slam the door shut, but it was too late. A large foot in an ugly brown shoe wedged itself firmly into the opening. And Wendell, the ghastly photographer from *Undercover USA*, wasn't far behind. He was wearing a bulky, greasy photographer's vest, and he had several different cameras strung around his neck. Nothing like announcing to the world at large who he was.

''Hey, Porter,'' he said with a smirk as he pushed his way inside. ''What's up?''

After a quick check of the hallway to make sure no one had spotted her suspicious visitor, Annie backed off to the other side of the room, near the windows. ''Keep your voice down,'' she hissed. She shut the window and pulled the drapes, just in case Trevor had the urge to come visiting. ''There's another contestant right next door.''

''Yeah, the guy, right?'' Wendell fixed her with an

unpleasant grin. "You two seem to be getting real cozy."

"At the press conference, you mean? That's nonsense," she said flatly. "I lost my balance for a minute. That's all."

"Uh-huh. Well, I got a great shot of the two of you that looks like a dynamite cover to me. Of course, the other one may be even better." He scratched his stubbled jaw. "You don't see guys like him carrying chicks down the street every day. The light wasn't as good on that one, plus I was farther away, but hey . . . all in all, it's a decent shot."

Annie went very still. "You saw us on the street? You took pictures?"

"Not much gets by me." Wendell smiled slyly. "That's my job."

This was rapidly turning into a nightmare. Annie tried desperately to think of a way to control this awful situation. The torchy photo from the press conference was one thing, but a clingy shot from their stroll down the Rue d'Anglais was quite another.

How would she explain that such a picture existed in the first place? It would blow her cover sky-high! Not to mention the fact that the photo undoubtedly placed them on the street outside the Framboise building when they weren't supposed to be there, which opened the door for somebody to trace them back to the stupid burglary scheme.

And then there was another problem.

Trevor would kill her if an incriminating photograph of the two of them appeared on the front page of *Undercover USA*.

Wendell plopped himself down on her delicate tapestried chair. "Now all I need is your story, Porter. You got it ready?"

That brought her back to reality. "What story?"

"*Your* story, Porter," he said loudly. "Something to go with my great pictures. How about 'Casanova Case falls hard for French prostitute, rescues her from the streets'? See, it fits right in.''

"That's a total lie.''

"Who cares? You're gonna be on the street if you don't come up with something, babe.'' He shook his greasy head. "The Big Toad is getting real antsy for some great stuff outa this, and pronto. Come on, it ain't so tough. You know the ropes: who's getting it on with who, how many broads the legal guy is making it with, any unusual places they're doing it . . . the normal stuff.''

"No one is doing anything with anyone,'' she said stiffly. She hated the ugly implications in Wendell's remarks, and yet she knew that he wasn't saying anything she hadn't heard a million times. Getting dirt was her job. Even if she couldn't face digging for it in this particular instance.

"So what if nothing's happened yet?'' Wendell returned. "All you gotta do is make up something then, right? You're the source, babe. This time we can back up anything we say, 'cause after all, we got an eyewitness. Hey, we can rearrange my photos to look like that Case guy is making it with all three of you, plus a monkey from the zoo, if that's the story you want. 'Romance Contest Turns into Paris Orgy.' Whaddya think?''

She thought he was disgusting. But sharing that opinion was probably not the best idea at the moment. She chewed a fingernail. "Wendell, about the pictures you took on the street . . . Please don't send those back to the Toad. Please?''

"Those may end up my best shots.''

"Look, I'll come up with something great to go with the other ones—the ones from the press conference. Something about Kerenza.'' She hoped she didn't sound too frantic. "Kerenza's a much better angle than I am. Who cares about pictures with me in them?''

"Yeah, well, that's true. No skin off my nose.'' He

shrugged, heaving himself up out of the chair. "Look, I gotta stop in some hole-in-the-wall town on my way back—I'm supposed to get some shots of the world's biggest bowling ball or something. So I won't be back at the office until the end of the week. If you've filed a story by then, I'll use it with one of my Kerenza pics, and nobody will see the other one. But if you don't come through, I'm going with what I got."

She had a week. It was a better deal than she'd expected. "I'll try," she said slowly.

"You better. When I left, the Big Toad was hopping. I go back and tell him I couldn't get squat outa you, plus you don't want me to use the pics I got, and he's gonna go through the roof. I'd start looking for another job if I was you."

"I can worry about that for myself, thank you," she told him. "Are you ready to go now, before someone sees you and blows my cover?"

"Yeah, yeah." He lumbered over to the door, and Annie began to breathe a sigh of relief. But then he turned back. "Almost forgot. I gotta go back tonight, so Toad said for you to take your own shots from here on," he said, pulling a tiny thirty-five-millimeter camera out of his gear bag. "All you gotta do is aim and shoot."

"Yeah, right."

He just stood there, holding it out, until she had no choice but to take the thing if she wanted to see the last of Wendell. With a frown, she stuffed it inside her purse. I may have it, but that doesn't mean I'm going to use it, she told herself.

Unfortunately, she wasn't sure she had a choice. If she didn't take the pictures and write the stories they wanted, she would find herself jobless, as well as on the front of the magazine, implicated in some smutty story, before the week was out.

And if she did the moral and ethical thing, and told C. Toad and his staff to take a flying leap, then she'd really be in hot water. She had no doubt that the Toad wouldn't stop at merely firing her. He'd rat on her, too, and tell everybody at Framboise that she was the lowest scum on earth. Marie-Ange, Jamie . . . and Trevor. They'd all know who she was and why she'd entered the contest.

"Hey, Porter, nothing but great stuff, right?" Wendell's beady eyes gleamed, as if he were imagining something really lewd. "Lots of flesh, lots of juice, in those stories. Go for it, babe."

And then, blessedly, Wendell was gone. She could only hope he'd be on the next plane back to the U.S.A., on to his photo opportunity with a giant bowling ball. She sure didn't want him anywhere near her.

"Oh, what's the use?" she asked out loud.

It wasn't Wendell she despised. It was herself, for contemplating, for even one minute, writing tattletale stories or snapping intimate photos of Trevor Case.

"I can't do it," she whispered. But what else was she going to do?

Trevor was in a very good mood. It hadn't taken more than a few phone calls to set up his "fantasy evening." After all, he'd done it once before.

Feeling very confident that the problem was now nicely disposed of, he wound his way back to the hotel in time to meet the others for a Framboise-sponsored dinner.

"You have several messages, Mr. Case," the concierge called out.

"Thank you," he said, with one of his better smiles, as he took the sheaf of papers. He stuffed them in his pocket, unwilling to ruin his mood by wading through a pile of notes from home. He expected them to be minor matters concerning cases and clients he could deal with when he got home.

Besides, a quick glance at his watch told him he'd better rush if he wanted to shower and change before dinner. And he did. Yes, he definitely wanted to spruce up, to hit Annie with every bit of well-dressed charm he had. Maybe he'd even have a chance to get a pretty little bouquet, fresh from the flower market at Place de la Madeleine.

Whistling "Isn't It Romantic?" in a jaunty rhythm, he raced up the ornate marble-paneled staircase. This contest wasn't turning out so badly after all. It had been unnerving to have to resort to common burglary to get a look at his essay, but even that had ended up okay, hadn't it? Not only had they gotten in and out with no adverse effects, but he'd had a chance to get a little closer to the adorable Annie. His smile widened as he remembered the look on her face when he'd carried her down the street in his arms.

Wonderful. That was a trip he wouldn't soon forget.

And now that the break-in was over, he had a decent fantasy on the horizon. Nothing spectacular, to be sure, but not terrible, either. That meant he would neither be found out as a fraud, nor be likely to win. All in all, the perfect situation.

Of course, there was the matter of Annie and her suspicions. She'd seemed very sure when she told him he couldn't possibly have written that essay. Hopefully, after a lovely, romantic evening on his yacht, any thoughts of turning him in would've vanished.

He kept whistling, feeling very optimistic about his prospects. Once he had her seeing things his way, he didn't think he'd have to worry about Annie.

His phone was ringing as he entered his room, and he picked it up before he even had a chance to turn on the light.

"Case, it's me, Pete," a curt voice said quickly. "I've been trying to get you all day."

"I just got my messages," he returned, thumbing through the sheaf of notes. Oddly enough, they were all from the same person, the guy who was now on the other end of the phone. It was Pete Brosnahan, the investigator Trevor used when he needed a little leg-work done, and the investigator he'd asked to look into Annie's background.

"I got the info you wanted on that Jonesborough woman. Hixville, Illinois, just like you said."

So far, so good. Trevor felt an immense rush of relief that she hadn't been lying.

"Born and raised in Hixville," Pete continued. "First in her class at Hixville High. Graduated 1988 from the University of Illinois, degree in journalism. Illinois driver's license, which, by the way, is expired, says she's five-one, a hundred one pounds, blond hair, blue eyes. Birthdate twelve–fifteen–sixty-five."

"Interesting, but not earthshaking. Anything else?"

"Oh, I got plenty," Pete said ominously. "Married, 1987, to a guy named Barry Alan Porter."

"Married?" he shot back. "Are you sure?"

"Absolutely." Sensing Trevor's discomfort, the P.I. chuckled dryly. "But don't sweat it, Case. She's di-vorced. Her ex is a lawyer, and doesn't sound like one of the better members of the species. As soon as he graduated from law school, he started divorce proceed-ings. She didn't even contest it, although God knows why. According to the settlement papers I've been able to get a look at, he got everything they had, every last dime, even though she put him through law school. Real nice guy. And it gets worse."

"Okay," he said. "What is it?"

"A kid."

Trevor closed his eyes. Annie with a child . . . "What happened?"

"I don't know," Pete told him, sounding uncharac-teristically confused. "There's some paperwork on a hearing regarding Chessy Porter, age three, but it's not called a custody hearing, so I don't really get it."

"Don't worry about what it was called. What hap-pened to the little girl?"

"Daddy got custody. He took a job at a fancy law

firm in Seattle, and took the kid with him. Your girl fought it tooth and nail, but she lost the kid.''

"No wonder she doesn't like lawyers," Trevor muttered. Outmanned and outmaneuvered, she'd probably never had a chance. Well, he thought with some arrogance, things might be different now that she had a high-powered attorney on her side. He might just offer his services to reopen that custody battle. And if he did, Barry Alan Porter would wish he'd never started this fight.

Pete added, "Yeah, well, she liked him well enough to keep his name.''

There was a pause. "What do you mean?" Trevor asked. "She's going by Jonesborough now. Anna Jonesborough.''

"If she is, it's kind of fishy," the P.I. advised. "Far as I can tell, she's been calling herself plain Annie Porter for the last eight years. It's on her lease, on her credit cards, and it's been her byline in the newspaper, if you can call that rag a newspaper, as recently as last week.''

He began to get a very funny feeling. "What rag?" he asked quietly.

"Undercover USA," Pete said casually, as though he weren't aware of the magnitude of the bomb he'd just dropped. "Your girl has been based south of Houston, writing for *Undercover USA,* for the past year and a half. I've got clippings of all kinds of stories she's done, if you're interested. Let's see, we've got Elvis sightings, Princess Di's new beau, a banana-and-peanut-butter-diet . . . Oh, and here's a good one.''

Trevor already knew what was coming.

"Annie Porter's byline is on the very first Legal Lothario feature," the P.I. said flatly. "The headline reads, 'Sable Malone's marriage goes kaput after she hires the Legal Lothario.' Remember that one?''

"Oh, yes," Trevor returned grimly. "I remember.''

EIGHT

Trevor kept watching her. Annie felt like a germ under a microscope as they made their way through another elaborate dinner thrown by the Framboise people.

After his behavior during the break-in, she'd expected something different from him. All those dazzling smiles, the devastating little nibble on her neck, and especially the ride down the street in his arms—it all added up to a romantic onslaught from the Legal Lothario.

Except that he'd never made another move.

As she eyed him, lounging down there at the other end of the dinner table, she wondered if she'd totally misread the situation, or perhaps taken some false step that had cooled his ardor. "Maybe it's all part of his plan," she whispered. "Running hot and cold, keeping me off balance."

She'd never been involved in a flirtation with a real live Casanova before. Maybe this was a normal step in the routine. If so, she wasn't planning on ever doing it again.

"I didn't plan on doing it in the first place," she reminded herself under her breath. Even if she weren't running out of time trying to meet Wendell's insane deadline, she wouldn't have had energy to spare for the likes of Casanova Case. "He's not my type, he's too arrogant by half, and he's a lawyer to boot. There's just no way I would've gone for his line."

Uh-huh. And pigs could fly.

"Annie, is something wrong?" Jamesina MacDougal asked kindly.

"No, of course not." She found a smile for the Scottish romance novelist, who continued to be the nicest person involved in the contest. If Marie-Ange was obsessive-compulsive, Kerenzà was a total dip, and Trevor Case was . . . well, whatever he was, at least Jamie MacDougal was a sweetheart. "Just mumbling to myself about how marvelous the food is."

Jamie gave her a dubious look. "All you have on your plate is a piece of bread."

Luckily Marie-Agne chose that moment to make a speech, diverting Jamie's attention. "Attention, everyone," the Framboise VP announced. "Monsieur Case has informed me that everything is ready, and his fantasy will take place tomorrow."

Annie sat up straighter. She hadn't heard a peep about Trevor's trip to Saint-Tropez since he'd asked her to come along, back in Marie-Agne's office. Was she still expected to participate? She'd said she would, but it hadn't been carved in stone. Given the way he'd been acting, maybe he no longer wanted her company in Saint-Tropez. And if he didn't, was that a reprieve? Or an insult?

She flashed him a surreptitious glance. He was staring at her again, measuring her with that steady gray gaze of his. When he looked at her like that, she always felt as if she'd been judged and found wanting. Defiantly she raised her chin and stared right back. *Take that, Casanova.*

Apparently not noticing the byplay between her contestants, Marie-Ange continued, "Monsieur Case has also informed me that Mademoiselle Jonesborough has agreed to accompany him."

Well, that settled that. But why? Why had he told Marie-Ange it was all set, trapping Annie into going, when he clearly couldn't stand the sight of her?

"The rest of us must content ourselves with their report of their evening together." The Frenchwoman honored them all with a bounteous smile. "Very romantic, yes?"

Trevor's chilly gaze didn't waver. Annie wanted to squirm. She wanted to shout, *Why do you want me to come with you if you dislike me so much?* She did neither.

And when he lifted his wineglass in a silent salute, she lifted hers, too.

"Annie," Jamie chided. "You never told me Trevor asked you to go along on his fantasy."

"I wasn't sure I was going," Annie said quietly.

"How could you pass that up?" Jamie asked.

"Good question." She needed to get a story, and it had to be done within the next four days, three hours, and twenty-six minutes, if her watch was right. That yacht off the Riviera sounded like a perfect opportunity to create some controversy *and* take some candid photos of Mr. Case. As long as he was mad at her, she might be able to work up enough righteous indignation to write something scandalous, to invade his privacy without a second thought.

Yeah, right. How was she going to manage that when she already felt guilty just thinking about it? She would deal with the guilt later, she told herself harshly. Right now she needed a story desperately.

And then there was the niggling little fact that deep in her heart, she really wanted to go. She really wanted to be alone with Trevor one more time.

She closed her eyes, remembering the feel of his lips brushing her neck, the feel of his long, lean body pressed up against her as he rubbed one of her own high heels up and down the curve of her bottom.

Traitorous memories. Traitorous heart.

At the other end of the table, Princess Kerenza asked loudly, "Why did you ask that little snippet of a girl, Trevor, darling? You two are always at daggers with each other."

"I prefer to know my enemies," Trevor said coldly. "At least I'll be able to keep an eye on her."

This time she went ahead and squirmed. "Looks like it's going to be a long night on that yacht," she murmured.

"A long night? You lucky dog," Jamie remarked with a knowing smile.

The date was going miserably. Trevor frowned, fiddling with the stiff tuxedo point of his collar. If he'd expected his little spy from *Undercover USA* to be seductive and sweet, in a clumsy attempt to weasel secrets out of him, he'd been sadly mistaken. Instead of Mata Hari, he was sharing the confines of this exquisite private train car with an ice princess.

It was supposed to have been a private jet, but he'd gone with the train instead, in deference to Annie's fear of flying. Not that she'd noticed, or shown the proper gratitude.

Ah well, he didn't expect gratitude. But he had been looking forward to the next step in her game, to gauge how he could twist it to his advantage. So far, there wasn't any game. Annie had been subdued and quiet, staring out the window of the train at the lights of the French countryside. What was wrong with her?

He was the one with a legitimate grievance. He felt like wringing her traitorous little neck every time he thought about the fact that she worked for that damn *Undercover USA*, writing lies about *him*. So what was *her* problem?

Things had gone wrong from the very first, when

he'd given her a dozen long-stemmed ivory roses, in keeping with the way he'd done this date the first time, so thoughtfully recorded in his nieces' entry. His companion on the first version of the trip, a leggy model named Shandy (who only had the one name), had squealed, "Wow! Just like Miss America. Cool!"

He didn't want anything so obvious from Annie, but one small smile might've been nice. But instead of pleased, Annie had just looked stricken.

"Don't you like roses?"

"No, they're beautiful," she'd assured him in a tiny voice, lumping them back into his arms as if they carried the plague. "But this is too much like a *real* romantic evening."

He handed the roses off to a kind porter, who found a vase for them, but the idea that she didn't appreciate his gesture still threw him. "Why isn't this a real romantic evening?"

"Real romantic evenings are between people who like each other," she pointed out delicately. "I don't think we count."

Unfortunately, he had no response for that one. *People who liked each other* didn't quite capture the strange relationship building between them. How about *people who lie to each other*? Or maybe *people who can't trust each other, but can't keep their hands off each other, either*?

Trevor regarded her moodily, tightening his fingers around the stem of his champagne flute. Sitting so serenely in one of the velvet love seats in the compartment's sitting room section, Annie looked sensational, much more tempting than the Framboise champagne or the chic hors d'oeuvres he was plying her with. She'd worn this luscious little dress, a tiny slip of a thing, in a kind of taupe silk that clung to her slender curves, hinting at the promise underneath. Her terrific legs were exposed past midthigh, and his eyes kept roaming over there, drinking in the sight of all that gorgeous flesh.

He swore under his breath. It wasn't fair for her to wear a dress like that and then act like Miss Frigidaire. He stopped himself before the fragile stem of the glass snapped in his rigid fingers. Instead, he poured himself a liberal amount of champagne. After all, they had buckets of the stuff, courtesy of Framboise International. Why not use it?

"More champagne, Annie?" he asked, trying out his slinkiest, most wicked tones. He might not consider himself a Casanova, but he knew the effect his voice had on women when he cared to use it.

"No, thank you," she returned politely, ignoring him *and* his voice.

"Annie," he said softly, edging over closer. "It's not going to be much of an evening if you won't talk to me."

Her eyes widened as he crept even nearer. He loved the look of anticipation, of heightened awareness, in her eyes. How long could she keep up the pretense that she didn't care that it was just the two of them, all alone, ensconced in the elegant little train car, rumbling along toward the south of France?

"Trevor," she began, and he waited, hoping she would say something provocative, something sexy . . . or at the very least, something hot-tempered, so they could get into a fight and blow off a little steam. "Trevor, why did you want me to come along on this date with you?"

The look in her soft blue eyes was so vulnerable, so hurt, that it took his breath away. "Why?" he repeated.

Because I wanted to punish you for lying to me? Well, that wasn't working out too well, was it? He was the one getting put through the wringer.

Maybe because my pride was wounded that you'd fooled me so easily. I wanted to see for myself if it could possibly be the truth. Funny, when he was in her company, it didn't seem to matter that she was a reporter for the sleaziest tabloid in America, that she probably had a tape recorder hidden in her bra and a camera tucked into her handbag. If he gave her the slightest opportunity, she'd make mincemeat out of his personal life and air his secrets in the most humiliating possible way.

But all he saw when he looked at Annie was the luminous light in her blue, blue eyes, the precarious way one of the straps of her dress slipped over her shoulder, the way a pale strand of hair curved across one cheek. What he saw was a woman he wanted. Badly.

Although he knew it was foolish, he told the truth. "I wanted to be alone with you."

"Alone?" she breathed. "With me?"

She seemed inordinately pleased. And so was he. A small smile danced across his lips as he reached out a hand, fingering the smooth curve of her cheek. "Yes, Annie," he murmured, brushing his thumb across the soft corner of her lips as she tipped up her face toward him.

Did she know how much he wanted to kiss her? God, he wanted to lose himself in her, to reach whatever it was that tantalized him, to solve this riddle once and for all.

"I could try some of that champagne now," she whispered.

A momentary reprieve. Only too aware that the evening was very young and full of promise, Trevor poured her a glass of the chilled, delicately pink champagne.

Her eyes sparkled as brightly as the crystal champagne flute as she smiled at him, and he found himself grinning back at her. For the moment, he put aside his questions and his anger, as well as his fierce need to touch her. His strategy for the evening disappeared like a wisp of smoke.

Instead of challenging her, instead of making her pay, he decided suddenly that he preferred to defuse her. With a bit of finesse, she and her tabloid games

could easily be circumvented, detoured, and derailed.
All he had to do was make her so occupied with some-
thing else that she forgot who she was for a few hours.
All he had to do was seduce her.

"A toast," he said, raising his glass. "A toast to a
lovely evening, and an even lovelier companion."

Blushing becomingly, Annie clinked her glass against
his. "To Paris, to train rides, and to Saint-Tropez."
She gave him a mischievous glance. "I can't wait to
see your yacht."

He was discovering that it was a lot more fun to be
on Annie's good side.

No doubt about it—Annie was having the time of
her life.

The stars twinkled overhead, as if they had been scattered in the sky just for the two of them. The polished
wood and brass of the racy little yacht gleamed in the
moonlight. They were anchored not far from the Saint-
Tropez harbor, but far enough to make it seem as
though they were very much alone.

Alone. With Trevor.

The very idea was enough to make her shiver where
she stood on the deck. Annie hoped she hadn't done
something very foolish. But if this was a bad move,
why did everything seem so right?

Back at the beginning of this evening, things had
been very different. When he'd picked her up, she'd
gotten one look at him, lounging there all tall and elegant in black tie, and she'd known she was in big trouble. Trevor was devastating enough in regular clothes,
but in a tuxedo, he was positively sinful!

And then he'd given her that big bunch of roses, and
every cynical thought she owned came back to haunt
her. It was like a fantasy, all right, but a big fat *fake*
fantasy, designed to win a contest, not a lady's heart.
Minutes from Paris, stewing over his damn tuxedo and

his damn roses, she'd wondered if she ought to toss herself off the train and get it over with.

But then he'd been so sweet, telling her he wanted to be alone with her. . . .

Her stomach flip-flopped just thinking of the heated expression in his eyes when he'd told her that. Annie took a deep breath. If he could bottle that expression, no woman in the world would be safe.

He really does want to be with me! That knowledge was much more potent than a gallon of Framboise champagne.

Not that the champagne hurt anything, either. They'd shared several glasses on the train, and then another glass before dinner. The wine, the food, and Trevor . . . Everything was conspiring to unwind her, to relax her defenses.

"Did I tell you I've never been on a yacht before?" she asked, bracing her elbows on the railing, gazing down into the deep, dark water that lapped at the sides of the boat.

"Only about a hundred times," he said indulgently.

"And dinner . . ." She glanced down, hoping her stomach didn't look too round under her rather revealing dress. Aw, who cared? "It tasted . . . wonderful," she said, savoring the memory of Bretonne lobster with artichokes and the way the delicious tastes had swirled around her tongue.

"I'm glad you liked it." He stood beside her on the deck, not touching, but very close. "That's my job— to make sure you enjoy yourself."

Job. Through her foggy brain, one idea penetrated. She'd almost forgotten, but her job depended on taking his photograph. "Trevor," she ventured, reaching for her purse, "would you mind if I took your picture? For a memento?"

After all, what harm could come to him if she snapped him looking great in his formal evening clothes? It wasn't anything shady, and C. Toad probably wouldn't even be able to use it. But at least she could say she'd sent him something.

He gave her a curious glance as she pulled out the tiny camera. "Why did you bring a camera along?"

"I want to remember the evening. And you," she improvised.

"You first. Then I'll pose for you." He smiled, but it was a strange, devious smile that didn't quite reach his eyes. "Here, give me the—"

He reached for the camera, but missed, knocking it clean out of her hand. Before she had a chance to react, the tiny camera sailed off over the side of the yacht and disappeared below the dark blue waves.

"Sorry," he offered.

"Oh, no," she groaned, searching the waves. Now she'd not only failed her assignment, but destroyed company property, too.

If she didn't know better, she'd have suspected he knocked it overboard on purpose. Trevor was not a clumsy man. Other than this little camera clash, she'd never seen him make a false move. But why would he purposely ruin her camera? Did he have a thing about getting his picture taken? Or was there something more to this?

"I would offer to dive into the drink and retrieve it for you," he murmured, staring at her with his most hypnotic gaze, "but I don't want to be away from you just now."

She forgot all about the camera.

Every word out of his mouth sounded sexy. It wasn't what he said; it was the hot light in his eyes and the husky note in his voice when he said it. His words seemed to tickle her senses, to sketch a lazy path up her bare back, where her dress dipped lower than it should've. Annie shivered again.

"Are you cold?"

"No. No, of course not." It was a mild, almost balmy evening, with only a slight, warm breeze. But even if it had been thirty degrees below zero, Annie doubted she would've felt the cold. No. Her internal thermometer was keeping her blazing.

He rested one warm, strong hand on her arm, gently rubbing her overheated flesh, and her whole body began to buzz and tingle. "You're trembling," he murmured. "You must be cold. Is there anything I can do to warm you up?"

God, he was good at this. She felt like a real amateur, out here in the moonlight with a man who'd had far too much practice acting irresistible. All she could think of to say was, "That might be nice."

Nice? What kind of a word was *nice*? What kind of dingbat was she, saying *nice* to Mr. Sophistication?

But it didn't matter. Nothing mattered when he bracketed her face with his elegant hands, gazing down at her with that rapt expression. All she could do was stare back at him, willing him to go ahead and kiss her before she died from unfulfilled desire.

"Annie," he murmured. "I haven't got a clue what I should do with you."

"Do with me?" she whispered back. "I think you should—"

But he cut off her words, lowering his lips to hers, singeing her with liquid fire.

His mouth was hot and demanding, sweet and seductive, all at the same time. She wound her arms around his neck, pulling him down to her, as her brain searched for some response more sensible than simply, mindlessly kissing him back.

But in the end, that was the only thing she could do, tangling her hands in the soft, dark hair at the nape of his neck, urging him on. She'd never been kissed like this before, and never felt such an immediate, incredible reaction. It was as if everything fell into place with one resounding crash of sensation.

His fingers traced the slick edge of her dress where it gaped in the back, barely grazing her skin, but driving her insane nonetheless. She felt so naked, so vulnerable, to his caress. Not cold, though. Anything but cold.

His lips left hers, dusting a trail of kisses down her neck and across her throat, across her chin and the corners of her mouth, until she was dying to taste him more completely. As if he knew what she wanted, he angled his lips across hers, taking his harsh, hot kiss deeper.

She edged herself as close as she could possibly get, sliding her silk-clad body against him all the way up and down. He was all muscle, all man, so hard and lean, so different from her. She pressed herself closer. But it wasn't close enough.

She was smoldering from the inside out, and the swirling, tantalizing pressure of his mouth only fueled the flames higher. All she wanted to do was get rid of her silly dress, tear him out of his tuxedo, and make love with him on the polished deck of the yacht.

Make love with him? Annie realized, in a sudden burst of clarity, that she had completely and irrevocably lost her mind.

"Trevor, wait," she managed, backing off just far enough to breathe, hopefully to restore some sense to her overcharged neurons. "We can't do this."

"Why not?"

Good question. Think fast, she ordered herself. "It's not in the script," she made up on the spur of the moment. ".And we have to go back and report on our evening. We can't report *this*."

He had her by the shoulders, and he showed no intention of letting her go. "Do you really think I would specify making love in my damn contest entry?" He was fuming. "I can't believe you think I'm such a creep that I'd report you to Marie-Ange for one perfectly innocent kiss."

"That was no innocent kiss, and you know it!" she shot back.

"What was so terrible about it? My mouth—your mouth—pressed very close together. Sounds about as normal as you can get to me."

She didn't know what to say. *If I kissed you any longer, my brain was going to explode* didn't seem to be the tactful way to go. Instead, she reached for a diversion. Anything to break this terrible tension.

"Weren't we supposed to take a moonlight swim? I seem to remember reading that in your essay. Maybe we should take our swim now."

He watched her under hooded lids, but then, wordlessly, Trevor retreated into the cabin, where they'd shared their romantic, gaslit dinner.

Whew. Annie sagged against the railing. That had been a close call.

"What could I have been thinking?" she berated herself. A casual kiss was one thing, even a cozy trip down the sidewalk in his arms . . . but a passionate embrace on board a ship, with nobody to rescue her if she got in over her head? Pure, unadulterated stupidity.

"Are you talking to yourself?" Trevor inquired as he strolled back out of the cabin. He was carrying a few scraps of bright-colored fabric. As he held up the tiny triangles of tropical-print material, she realized it was a bathing suit. A very skimpy bathing suit.

"You don't expect me to—to—" she sputtered.

There was a flicker of mischief in his eyes, but Trevor only shrugged. "You're the one who requested a swim. You certainly aren't dressed for it at the moment."

"Well, I'm not wearing that thing."

"Did you bring a suit?" he asked, all innocence. "Or do you want to skinny-dip?"

Annie choked in midbreath. "Skinny-dip?" Quickly she grabbed the bathing suit and headed for the bathroom. Swimming in a suit as tiny as this one was still preferable to standing on a deck in the moonlight with

Trevor. At least she'd be neck-deep in cool water. Not so different from taking a cold shower, after all.

The shipboard bathroom was microscopic, and it was hard to wiggle out of her panty hose and into that mini-suit when she kept banging her elbows on the sink and knocking her knees on the door. Finally she had wrestled the pieces into place. But she took one good look down, and said, "No way." This wasn't a swimming suit—it was three postage stamps with a little string in between!

Tugging here and there in an unsuccessful attempt to be more modest, Annie made her way cautiously around the cabin and across the deck, turning out lights as she went. No need to illuminate her embarrassment.

Trevor did not appear in her path, for which piece of luck she was eternally grateful. In a race to get into the safe cover of the water before he saw her, she crept down the ladder over the side of the boat, jumping off the last rung with a discreet splash.

"I'm in," she announced, happily paddling away.

The water was cool and refreshing, knocking away the cobwebs and making her feel like she could think again. It was terrific to forget her worries and just relax, leaning back into the gentle waves.

"Going in first is cheating, Annie," he called out from above her. She couldn't see him up there very well—it was too dim—but she definitely caught the motion when he dove off the deck. His lean, perfect body glistened in the moonlight, slicing into the water about five feet away from her.

"Isn't that dangerous?" she demanded when he surfaced.

"Only if you don't know what you're doing." He shook his head, sending droplets flying in a wide arc.

Annie swam a few strokes farther away, but he followed, diving under and catching her ankle as she tried to escape. He hauled her back up against him.

"No fair," she said breathlessly, pushing off with a

splash, but Trevor clearly didn't care about what was fair.

Everything was slippery and different under the surface of the water. Suddenly her cool little sojourn in the surf was every bit as tense as their clinch on deck.

As he swam out and around her, playing at cat and mouse, she felt his hand touch hers, his leg slip past her thigh. She feinted one way while he went the other, but he was too quick, too smart. Just when she thought she was safe, he caught her. His arms were around her, holding her close, and her almost naked chest bumped squarely against his. She could feel her breasts rising and falling, threatening to spill out of the insufficient covering of the bikini top, as she tried to catch her breath.

But Trevor wasn't looking down there. No, he was gazing straight into her eyes.

The water was cool, but his arms around her were very warm. She had the urge to melt into him, to plaster herself up against him, to experience his wonderful heat again.

It was dark and tricky navigating these waters, and Annie once again felt out of her depth.

"Well, that's enough for me," she said in a rush. She flashed away, bursting up out of the water, grabbing for the ladder, escaping from Trevor's grasp by the skin of her teeth. Without looking back, she climbed up and over, and then raced across the deck to a big pile of towels.

Hurriedly she wrapped herself in three huge beach towels, covering every inch of her skin. She also turned on every lamp on the boat, shattering the darkness with harsh light.

No more of these games. She was going to be completely protected.

Trevor spent a few extra moments in the water below, but then he, too, returned to the boat. Standing there, dripping in the barely respectable swimsuit, with his broad shoulders, his smooth, muscled chest, and his long, strong legs very much revealed, he looked gorgeous.

She wished fervently she still had the camera. Now, *this* was something to record for posterity.

"Here you are, all covered up already," he said mockingly. "Didn't you like the suit?"

She felt her cheeks color. It was really a pain to be so fair-skinned that any little upset gave her a raging blush. "It wasn't big enough," she told him, sinking down inside her terry cloth tent.

"A girl twice your size wore it the last time," he teased. "Shandy didn't have any problem with it."

Annie went stock-still. "Shandy?" she asked quietly. "As in Shandy, the fashion model who is six feet tall and keeps marrying rock stars? She wore this suit, on this yacht, with you?"

She could tell from the look on his face that he knew he'd made a mistake.

"She was on this yacht?" she demanded again.

He shrugged. "She came here once. It was no big deal."

But Annie was beginning to get the picture. In fact, she was beginning to feel like Conquest number 983 in the little black book of Casanova Case. She hadn't been chosen for any reason in particular, but simply because she was female and she was available.

What else could explain the disparity—in height and status and celebrity, and certainly in IQ—between her and Shandy, the pea-brained model who wore bathing suits for a living? Annie had been very unsure of her appeal to begin with, and now all those old doubts came back to plague her.

"So this date, this romantic evening with an awesome babe—it's a rerun, isn't it?"

"Well, yes, I suppose, but—"

"Don't tell me, let me guess. Some roses, some hors d'oeuvres, and maybe a few glasses of champagne. And after that, a nice, cozy dinner for two. Bretonne lobster with artichokes, perhaps? No dessert, but a midnight swim. Maybe she was a little more receptive than I've been, once you got her stripped to the bikini. Is that right?''

"Annie," he protested, but she had already swept past him, intent on retrieving her dress, stuffing herself back into her panty hose, and getting off this damn boat as soon as possible.

"I think your romantic evening just came to an end, Case. Your 'awesome babe' is taking a powder.''

NINE

"So," Marie-Ange began, with more than a hint of curiosity in her voice, "did you enjoy your rendezvous with Monsieur Case?"

"It was nice."

Marie-Ange cocked an eyebrow. "That is hardly a ringing endorsement, Miss Jonesborough."

Annie tried to sound more convincing. "It was *very* nice."

"Hmmm." The Framboise VP made a few notes on a paper in front of her. "Go on, please."

Annie hoped she wasn't blushing. She'd come in here trying to be fair, to paint an adequate picture of Trevor's achievement. After all, except for one snafu, his efforts had succeeded admirably. And she was determined not to behave like some pitiful woman scorned, not to be petty or jealous, and to get out of Marie-Ange's office without anyone the wiser as to what had really happened.

But Marie-Ange kept poking. "Miss Jonesborough? I must know, for the report, more details."

Annie stalled for time. "What would you like to know?"

"Take me through the entire evening." Marie-Ange smiled. "Start at the beginning."

In a rush, she announced, "Well, he picked me up at the hotel, and he was dressed formally. Let's see, he was wearing a black dinner jacket, black tie, a white tuxedo shirt, black studs. He looked . . ." She swallowed, but then forced herself to keep going. Details. They were just mindless details, and they couldn't faze her. "He looked very nice, as I'm sure you can imagine. Mr. Case is a very handsome man, after all, and in formal wear, well, he looked . . ."

She hurried on. "He had roses for me, white roses, a big bunch of them. We took a train out of Paris. It was a private train car, kind of old-fashioned-looking, with etched glass windows and velvet settees."

"Mmmm. Atmosphere," Marie-Ange murmured.

"Yes, it was nice."

"And?" Marie-Ange prompted.

She felt like a robot, but she charged along as best she could. "We had champagne and hors d'oeuvres on the train. Framboise Champagne, of course, and a little caviar, some truffles, some little tart things. It was—"

"Nice, I suppose," the Frenchwoman supplied dryly. "And after the train?"

"He'd arranged a car to take us to the harbor at Saint-Tropez, where the yacht was waiting."

"Yes, yes. And then?"

"Dinner. On the yacht. Bretonne lobster with artichokes." She'd memorized that much. "More champagne, of course. The food was marvelous." At least she could summon some enthusiasm for that. "After dinner, we took a swim in the moonlight, and I guess that's everything." She stood to leave.

"Please." Marie-Ange pointed to the chair. "I'm not finished."

She wasn't volunteering anything, so she waited for another question.

"Was it romantic?"

"Yes."

"Did he kiss you?"

Annie chewed her lip. "Is this really part of the report?" she asked finally.

Madame Vice President shrugged. "I am trying to gauge how romantic it was. The mood, the atmosphere . . . it is all important."

"The mood and the atmosphere were just great. Moonlight on the water, champagne, these kind of dim brass lamps all over the boat—very romantic."

"And then he kissed you?"

Oh, brother. "Yes, he kissed me," she mumbled.

"Where?"

She felt hot color suffuse her cheeks. "On the lips," she managed.

"No, no," the other woman returned impatiently. "Where on the boat?"

"Oh, I see. On deck, in the moonlight."

"Mmmm. Lovely," said Marie-Ange, as if that's exactly what she was hoping to hear.

Annie got the distinct impression her French companion was enjoying this as a vicarious thrill. This had to be the first time in Annie's memory that anyone was looking at *her* love life as a model of excitement. But why not? The kiss, the sexy swim, Trevor wearing hardly any clothes . . . it was pretty good stuff to build a night of fantasies on.

"So, all in all, you would give the evening high marks as a romantic fantasy?"

"Oh, yes," she said softly, before she had a chance to stop herself. Suddenly she was submerged in a kaleidoscope of images . . . the taste of his mouth, the feel of his hand on her bare shoulder, the wet, slippery flash of his thigh on hers. She was overheated all over again.

"Hmmm," Marie-Ange murmured, breaking the reverie. "Perhaps so. But you returned to Paris alone, isn't that right? You came back on the train several hours ahead of Monsieur Case."

"Well, yes, but—"

"And why is that? Shouldn't such a romantic interlude have involved a more tender parting of the ways?"

"I suppose, but . . . well, I was tired. I was ready to come home."

"And Monsieur Case wasn't?"

"I guess he was. I don't really know." She braved it out. How Marie-Ange knew that they'd parted acrimoniously, she had no idea. Spies, no doubt. "He was still taking care of the yacht when I left, you know, polishing all that brass, dropping anchor, cutting his jib, folding his sails. . . ." Were there sails? She hoped Marie-Ange didn't understand enough to call her bluff. "I just took the next train. I guess I thought the fantasy part was over."

"Hmmm," the vice president said again, scribbling more notes into her file. And then she looked up, sending Annie a piercing stare. "Are you sure that's all?"

But Annie didn't know what else to say. *I found out about the girl who came before me, and bolted* was hardly complimentary to either of them.

Thankfully, Marie-Ange's assistant, Bertrand, intervened, sticking his head around the doorframe. "I regret interrupting," he said hurriedly. "So sorry. But there is an important message for Miss Jonesborough from the United States."

"A message? For me?"

"*Oui.* Your brother, Todd, has just called."

She didn't have a brother. And she knew only one person named Todd—C. Todd Entwhistle, her boss. A quick glance at her watch told her she still had a good two days and six hours to go until she hit Wendell's deadline. Nonetheless, she sensed she was in deep trouble. "He called here?"

"*Oui,*" Bertrand said again. "The message is: 'Why have we not heard from you? Please send us word immediately.' You understand?"

Annie nodded. She wished she didn't understand.

"All right then," Marie-Ange said officiously. "You may go and make your call. Thank you, Miss Jonesborough."

"Right." She was up and ready to scuttle out of there in thirty seconds flat.

Unfortunately, she smacked headlong into Trevor Case, who was waiting to come in. The minute she bumped him, hip to hip, her body snapped to attention. She tried to change direction, to push away from his overpowering touch, but that only made things worse.

Attempting to wedge past him, she became hopelessly entangled between him and the wall, with one of the buttons on the front of her dress twisted around his cuff link. *Good grief!* How did that happen? She wrenched away, not caring if she lost the button and ripped her dress, but the fabric held, almost knocking them both over in the process.

"Steady," he said, keeping his free arm wound tightly around her. He paid no attention to the cuff link problem, and they both knew why. Because he liked the feel of his hand there, only inches from the curve of her breast. And so did she.

"Let me go," she muttered.

Slowly, maddeningly, he untangled her button, somehow managing to take forever, and to rub the heel of his hand against her neckline, ever so slightly, even though he seemed so intent on the task. Then he had the audacity to brush off the front of her dress, as if the collision had somehow mussed her outfit. His long, clever fingers barely grazed her buttons, but they left a devastating imprint nonetheless.

There was a calm, measuring look in his eye when he asked, "All finished with your report?"

"Yes." Between clenched teeth, she seethed, "Don't worry. I lied. I told her it was all terrific and we had a great time."

He smiled, with a flash of arrogance and charm. "All for naught, Annie. I'm going to tell the truth. It was a miserable excuse for a romantic encounter, and I failed completely at creating a memorable evening.''

He was even more insufferable when he was being noble. Intending to deflate a little of that self-assurance, Annie inquired, "And are you planning to mention the fact that you didn't write your own essay in the first place?"

There was a pause. "And who would've written it, if I didn't?"

Annie raised her chin. "I don't know yet. Your secretary, maybe. Someone under twenty-one, that's for sure."

"Annie," he said, in a very cold voice, "I hope you haven't been sharing your nonsensical theories with anyone else." His voice got even lower, more deadly. "You haven't told anyone, have you?"

"Marie-Ange, you mean? No, I haven't," Annie returned, crossing her arms over her chest. "But I should've."

"You would've looked like a fool if you had." Looking decidedly more relieved, he raised an eyebrow. "After all, who else could've written it? As you very well know, I'm the one who lived it before. Or have you forgotten about Shandy?"

She blushed furiously. Clearly he was trying to sidetrack her by making her angry again. She hated being so predictable. "How could I forget about Shandy?"

"I don't know, but I wish you would." He moved to enter Marie-Ange's door, but Annie pulled his sleeve.

"Trevor . . ." She didn't know quite how to phrase this. "You aren't going to say anything about . . . the more personal moments, are you?"

"Good grief, Annie," he muttered. "I would never even consider betraying anything private that happened between us. Unlike some people I could mention."

"Are you talking about me?" she asked suddenly. "You think I would . . . ?"

She was wounded. How could he think so little of her? She would never, *never* . . .

But of course she would. That was her job, after all. After all, her story deadline loomed, only a few days away. And to satisfy that deadline, she had been considering—and was still considering—doing exactly what Trevor had implied. But how did he know that?

Panic seized her. Trevor didn't know, did he? No, he couldn't. She couldn't stand it if he did.

"Why did you say that?" she demanded. "Just to make yourself feel better when you spill your guts to Marie-Ange? You're planning on telling her everything, down to the damn string bikini, aren't you?"

Trevor shook his head. "I can't believe this," he muttered. "I'm completely innocent, and you're standing there, as guilty as sin. So why am I the one taking all the hits?"

"Completely innocent? What about Shandy?" Her head was whirling. "And why am I as guilty as sin? What's that supposed to mean?"

But he didn't respond, just swept into Marie-Ange's office, leaving Annie standing in the hall seething. What was he talking about? Surely the great Trevor Case wasn't simply suffering from hurt pride that she'd walked out on him. Could he be so angry that he would label her impromptu departure from the boat a *sin*?

It just didn't add up. But the only other possibility was that he knew about her ties to *Undercover USA*.

He could be in Marie-Ange's office right now, spilling the beans, unmasking Annie as a fraud and a traitor. Her blood ran cold at the very thought.

"He can't know," she whispered. "If he did, he wouldn't save it for Marie-Ange. I know him; he couldn't resist confronting me. He'd slap me down with that information so fast, my head would spin."

She only hoped she was right.

* * *

"Telephone messages, mademoiselle," the concierge called out, but Annie kept on walking.

Ever since the message from C. Todd, taken while she was in Marie-Ange's office, she'd been inundated with phone calls and telegrams. At least she hadn't seen Wendell again, lurking around with his camera, so she assumed he'd been telling the truth when he said he was headed home to photograph bowling balls.

But how long would it take before the Toad sent someone else? Or, God forbid, showed up himself? There was also a distinct possibility that he would just fire her long distance.

She had to think of some way to circumvent this, to soothe her boss and keep her job, without writing anything trashy about the contest (or admitting that the camera they'd given her was now at the bottom of the Mediterranean), and without letting on to Trevor that she was connected to the tabloid. If he didn't know already . . .

It was hopeless.

"Someone is certainly trying hard to reach you," Jamesina MacDougal commented. "What's this all about?"

Annie pretended not to understand. "Pardon?"

"Everyone keeps shouting at you that you have urgent messages from the States, and you keep avoiding reading them." Jamie caught at Annie's arm, halting her progress through the lobby. "What's going on?"

"Nothing important." She lifted her hands, poohpoohing the whole thing. "I know what the messages are—it's this silly mess that cropped up at my old job back home—and I don't want to deal with the hassle right now, that's all."

"Okay," Jamie said dubiously. "This doesn't have anything to do with your lovers' quarrel with Trevor, does it?"

"There is no quarrel with Trevor, lovers' or otherwise," Annie maintained. She strode out the lobby door and onto the sidewalk, peeved enough to leave Jamie trailing behind. Which was worse, talking about her lousy job back home, or rehashing her horrid date with Trevor? It was a toss-up.

"Annie, I just don't believe you," Jamie maintained. Catching up, she steered her in the other direction. "I can still see sparks."

"Baloney," Annie returned sharply. "I know you think it would be really exciting and romantic if we fell madly in love during the contest, but it isn't going to happen. We're oil and water, polar opposites, David and Goliath."

"I don't think that one fits."

"It doesn't matter," she said stubbornly. "I'm just not cut out for playing footsie with a Casanova. You never know what to believe, or whether you can trust them." She shook her head vigorously. "Not this girl."

"But, Annie, Trevor's no Casanova. I'm a very good judge of character, and I can tell that he has integrity and warmth." Jamie smiled mistily. "Real hero material."

"Good judge of character? You're a total romantic," Annie scoffed. "You're imagining Romeo and Juliet under every tree. But this time, you're barking up the wrong Juliet."

"If you say so," Jamie said darkly, in a tone that telegraphed just how unconvinced she remained. "But are you going to be able to enjoy our shopping trip with this on your mind?"

"This is my first chance for real, live, honest-to-goodness tourist stuff. You bet I'm going to enjoy it." Annie smiled grimly. "I want to see every café, every bistro, every bookstore, every museum, I can squeeze in."

"I'm afraid there isn't a lot of time for that," Jamie reminded her. "I only got us excused from the usual press appearances by telling Marie-Ange I needed the time to pick up a few things for my fantasy. You're supposed to be helping.''

''I know, I know. But how long can a few things take?''

''Well,'' Jamie said pensively, checking her list as they neared the metro stop, ''there's the vintage lingerie shop and an antique store in Saint-Germain. This man swears he has a brass hip bath, or at least I hope that's what he said. And then we need to pop over to the Ile Saint-Louis, where I've made an appointment to see the costumer I'm using. The man who's arranging for me to use his country house is also on Saint-Louis, so hopefully we can take care of that as well.''

''Costumes? Country houses?'' Annie asked in disbelief. This was the second time Jamie had dropped hints about her fantasy. ''What in the world have you cooked up? This sounds like something by Agatha Christie. You know, *Murder at the Vicarage* or something, with everybody in clerical collars and sturdy tweeds.''

''Oh, no, nothing like that,'' Jamie murmured, hurrying down the stairs to the subway.

Annie peppered her friend with questions, but Jamie refused to discuss it as she purchased their metro tickets, and then guided Annie through the turnstile.

''I'm really glad you know what you're doing,'' Annie remarked, following Jamie's lead by sticking her ticket into a slot in the turnstile, retrieving it when it popped back up, and then clanking through the gate. ''All of this is new to me.''

''I love Paris,'' Jamie responded happily. She braced open the heavy door to the subway car as Annie sneaked in.

With a small sigh of relief, Annie dropped into the seat next to Jamie. She always got a little anxious when she was trying new things. ''You're very good at all this. You must've visited Paris a lot.''

''Oh, no, never. This is my first trip.''

Annie's eyes widened. ''But you act like a native.''

Jamie smiled placidly as she pulled a metro map out of her purse. "I doubt the natives would agree with you. My French accent is deplorable, as I've been told more times than I care to admit. But I believe in just plugging along and paying no attention." She frowned down at the map. "I know they'll understand me sooner or later if I keep asking."

"But how do you know your way around so well?"

"I've done lots of research," Jamie explained. "I set a three-book series during the French Revolution, so I had to sound like I knew my way around Paris. At the time, I couldn't afford to visit, so I ended up with a whole set of fabulous maps. I have everything from the latest, most detailed metro guides to an authentic eighteenth-century street map."

"How would you get a thing like that?"

"I've been corresponding with a gentleman who runs this lovely map store on the Left Bank, not far from the lingerie shop we're visiting." Jamie brightened as the subway car screeched to a stop. "Here we are."

Annie tagged along after her friend, amazed at how easy Jamie made things. Alone in Paris with only a map, Annie would've been intimidated and anxious. But Jamie breezed along, pointing out the hotel where Oscar Wilde died one moment, and a Picasso sculpture the next. Down alleys and narrow, tree-lined streets they forged, headed straight for whatever goal Jamie had in mind. Everyone should have a fearless tour guide like Jamie on their first trip to Paris.

"Voilà!" Jamie exclaimed, really getting into the spirit of things with this display of impromptu French. Eagerly she turned off a cobblestone street and in at a small, hole-in-the-wall boutique, whose front window was a waterfall of creamy silks and frothy lace.

"What are we doing here?" Annie asked, eyeing a fragile camisole with interest. Clearly this was the lingerie store Jamie had spoken of. Its wares were beautiful, but what part did lingerie play in Jamie's fantasy?

Jamie didn't answer; she was too busy gesticulating and spouting a jumble of French at a stout old woman who appeared to be the proprietor of the store. At one point, both Jamie and the shopkeeper appeared to be discussing Annie, frowning at her, surveying her up and down, which was even more mystifying.

"Why are you looking at me?" she asked, but they had swept on to something else by then.

"Bon!" Jamie said suddenly. "Yes, yes, exactly. *Exactement, vous comprenez?"*

The woman just stood there, hands on hips, shaking her head at the folly of people who massacred her native language. But finally she muttered, in heavily accented English, "Okay, okay. I try." And then she began to bustle around in a nearby trunk that overflowed with dainty things.

First she held up a heavily boned pink brocade corset, but Jamie sneered at it. "That's from the eighteen nineties. Not good enough, madame. Not nearly good enough."

"Not good enough?" The woman threw up her hands and started to curse at them in rapid French, but Jamie was implacable.

After a string of epithets, the woman eventually took out a small key and opened a different trunk, from which she gingerly pulled the oddest-looking corset Annie could've imagined. For one thing, it laced in both the front and the back, and for another, it was very skinny and rather long, with a high, tight bodice. It angled severely to a nipped-in waist, with a sort of little peplum popping out under that. It looked like a flea might fit in it comfortably, but that was about it.

The woman carrying the contraption bore down on Annie with a grimly determined expression.

"Oh, no," she cried, backing up.

But the stout shopkeeper was quicker than she looked. Before Annie knew it, the burly woman had slung the corset around her for a trial fit.

"C'est bon," she huffed, wresting Annie's arms out to the sides and squeezing the thing around her.

"Why are you trying this on me?" Annie demanded. She gasped, holding her breath painfully as the corset pinched her into submission.

"Perfect," Jamie said happily. "Now, what about the chemise? Oh, and hoops, of course, or a farthingale, or whatever's right for the period. And a silk nightdress . . ." She sighed with happiness. "Isn't this great, Annie?"

"Dandy."

Thank goodness she was speedily released from that torture chamber of a corset. She had no problem with Jamie enjoying herself, and enjoy herself, she did, as they tripped from one merchant to the next, looking at exquisite hand-embroidered linens here and antique jewelry there.

"Everything is going to be perfect," Jamie said happily, but Annie was beginning to get a very bad feeling about all of this. And when the man at the costume shop, deep in the bowels of a strange old theater, pulled out a tape measure and started her way, the bad feelings erupted into a symphony.

"Jamie," she ventured, "I've already figured out that you're doing some sort of costume ball thing. But you're not expecting me to play the lead, are you?"

"As a matter of fact, I was hoping you would," Jamie admitted. "I'm in a bit of a bind, Annie, and there's no one else. I thought today was a good opportunity to perhaps talk you into it."

"But you've already had everything sized for me! What were you going to do if I said no?"

Cheerfully Jamie told her, "I knew you wouldn't turn me down."

Getting crankier by the minute, Annie batted away the helpful little man with the tape measure. "Why can't *you* do it? It's *your* fantasy."

"Oh, but that would never work," Jamie said

blithely. "I know exactly what's going to happen, and the most intriguing part of my fantasy is the element of surprise. Plus it's important that the girl not speak French. You're the only person I know in Paris who doesn't speak French."

"Jamie!" she protested. "This isn't fair!"

"You'll love it," Jamie promised. "I certainly wish I could do it myself, because it's going to be so incredibly fabulous. If I could, I would. But I can't. That would spoil it. So you'll have to. Really, Annie, you'll love it."

By consenting to let herself be measured, she knew she was as good as giving in, but she couldn't hold the pesky little man off any longer. Besides, what would it hurt?

"Maybe I'll do this," she decided. "Maybe. But first you have to give me more of an idea what I'm getting into."

"But I can't. I told you, it's important that it be a surprise."

"You haven't signed me up for anything kinky, have you?" Annie asked suspiciously. "No Dracula's castle or the Marquis de Sade capturing virgins, or anything like that?"

"Of course not!" Jamie said indignantly. "What do you take me for? This is supposed to be romantic, not scary. After all, I write *romance* novels. As it happens, my books are very popular. I'm an expert at this sort of thing."

"Are you sure?"

"Positive!"

She had one other niggling suspicion, based on the fact that Jamie had a matchmaking streak a mile wide, and kept harping on the fact that Trevor and Annie had "sparks." "If you want me to be the heroine at your costume ball, who've you got lined up to be the hero of this little adventure?"

"In the first place, I never said it was a costume ball," Jamie said with a frown.

"Okay, okay," she agreed, even though she was very sure Jamie was bluffing, and when all was said and done, she would find herself waltzing around like Cinderella. But who was lined up for Prince Charming? "Tell me who the hero is," Annie insisted.

"Nobody you know," Jamie answered vaguely. "Let's see, I've got his name somewhere. Ah, yes, here it is. Jean-Pierre Billaud, the Duke of Varenne."

"A duke? A real one? Where did you dig up a duke?"

Jamie waved a dismissive hand. "There are scads of them bopping around Europe. Dukes, princes, counts . . . a whole assortment."

A fantasy in a posh country house with a duke as her date . . . Well, it would be a diversion, if nothing else.

"And I'm not expected to get interested or do anything with this guy, right? I mean, this isn't a blind date or anything?"

"Of course not."

"Well, okay," she murmured, envisioning herself in a trailing ball gown, lilting around a ballroom on the arm of a duke. "Maybe I'll do it."

"Wonderful, wonderful!" Jamie exclaimed, dancing over and hugging Annie, oblivious to the man with the measuring tape. "You're going to be so glad you agreed."

Obligingly Annie lifted her arms and let the man wrap his tape around her bodice. "Why do I get the feeling I've just been conned?"

TEN

The telephone was ringing. Annie woke up with a start, in the middle of a very strange dream, something about swimming in the ocean wearing nothing but a corset. The next moment she was bolt upright in her bed, listening to the blare of the phone.

Still disoriented, she gave in and reached over, feeling blindly for the receiver. But then she realized. Giving out a little squeal of dismay, she snatched her hand away as if the phone were on fire.

"I know it's you, Toad," she announced. Groaning loudly, she leaned back into the bed and shoved a pillow over her head. "And I have no intention of listening to you read me the riot act this early in the morning."

But how long could she go on like this? Ever since Wendell's visit, she'd been tossing out her messages, not answering the phone, and in general, acting like a coward. How long could she ignore the clarion call of the real world? Especially while the damn phone kept ringing!

She glanced at the clock. Seven-thirty A.M. This was her last day. By the end of this afternoon, Wendell would turn in the terrible photos.

Clearly the thing to do, to solve all of her problems in one fell swoop, was to sit down and come up with a story to send back to the Toad. She was a writer, and a good one. One simple story shouldn't be so tough, should it? Of course, she'd been wracking her brain for a story all week, and so far had come up with absolutely nothing, but still . . .

"I don't even like Trevor Case," she said bravely. "He's a cad and a heartbreaker, and all I have to do is share with the world exactly what he's like."

Of course, to do that, she would have to form at least one coherent thought, which at the moment seemed impossible. If only the lousy telephone would just shut up! Annie tossed back the covers and marched into her marble bathroom, securely shutting the door on the incessant ringing in the other room. Surely she could think up something good locked in the relative peace of the shower.

"Casanova Case Gets the Cold Shoulder," she cooked up, as the first spray of water hit her face. As a headline, it wasn't too bad. She searched for the next line. "Trevor Case has tried all of his wiles, but the women of France are too smart for him. Although he has apparently tried to romance everyone from the hotel maid to our own *Undercover* reporter, our sources indicate that Mr. Case, also known as the Legal Lothario, will return to the U.S. unloved and unwanted. Is this the end of the road for this Casanova without a clue?"

Annie laughed out loud, but water dripped in her mouth, making her sputter. Okay, so calling him a bust in the love department was pretty funny, but would anybody be interested in reading it? Not likely. *Undercover USA* readers were predictable, after all. They wanted Elvis alive, and they wanted their Legal Lothario still knocking 'em dead.

Annie shampooed her hair, grasping at straws. How about CASANOVA CASE ROMANCES SECRETARY TO RIP OFF HER BOSS? She could do a story about the break-in at the Framboise office, including a few concocted quotes from a mysterious inside source at the company, who would sobbingly report, *He told me he loved me, but all he wanted was a look at the files!*

"Get real," Annie chastised herself as she rinsed out the bubbles. "It's too stupid, too mean, and downright boring besides. Who cares if he steals something as mundane as a couple of sheets of paper? Plus he'd know in a minute I had to be involved, since I was the only other one there."

She concentrated harder. "Think," she commanded herself. "How about Kerenza? Surely you can come up with something unpleasant about her."

Princess Kerenza's Secret Lover: Is her trip to Paris really just an excuse for a Royal Rendezvous?

"Oh, brother!" Annie moaned. "That's downright pitiful."

She heaved a big sigh and leaned against the cool marble wall of the shower. Deep in her heart, she knew this wasn't working. All of her ideas were simply dreadful, and they were going to continue to be dreadful until she faced reality.

She hated her job. She just couldn't do it anymore. And that fact meant that there wasn't going to be any story, not about Kerenza, not about the contest, and certainly not about Trevor.

"He may be a rat, but even he doesn't deserve *Undercover USA*. And he may be a rat, but—" it was hard to admit the rest, even to herself "—I like him."

He was a difficult person to dislike. If only he were stupid, or pompous. Or just a little ugly. But no! He had to be smart and funny and absolutely gorgeous. Just to plague her.

She tried to remind herself that he'd played her for a fool, coming on to her in the exact same way, no doubt down to the color of the roses, that he'd already tried on Shandy, the six-foot-tall bimbo with more hair than brains. He was arrogant, he was overwhelming, and he was too sexy for his own good, let alone hers.

But it didn't matter. What mattered was that he had a way of getting under her skin, of making her feel like *she* was the one who wasn't being fair. How had he managed all that in so short a time?

"God, he's good. Too good," she muttered. But there was no time for that now. She had just decided what she was going to do.

As she toweled off, she realized that the phone was no longer ringing in the bedroom. Perfect. Quickly she hustled in there, still wearing the towel, and dialed down to the front desk.

"Mademoiselle Jonesborough, you have many messages," the clerk said immediately. "You must answer them, please, or we will not be responsible."

"Tear them up," she said impatiently. "Throw them away. All of them."

"Are you quite sure?"

"Positive. Now, here's what I need you to do." She held the receiver in one hand and hitched her towel up with the other. "I want you to send a telegram, right away, to Mr. C. Todd Entwhistle, care of *Undercover USA*, Jenkins Island, Texas."

After a moment, during which she heard the frantic rustle of pens and paper, the clerk said, "Yes, mademoiselle? And the message?"

A thrill of excitement, of anticipation at the enormity of what she was about to do, zinged through her veins. She took a deep breath, and then she said it.

"I quit."

As soon as the two small words were past her lips, a heavy burden was lifted from her heart. She felt like singing it at the poor desk clerk.

"Have you got that?" she asked. "I said, 'I quit.' "

"*Oui*, mademoiselle. To Mr. C. Todd Entwhistle: I quit. Is that all?"

"Yes," she assured him as her lips curved into an irrepressible smile. "That's it."

She now had no job, no good reason to think she'd be the one who got the Romance Ambassador post, and no other prospects. But who cared?

Her smile grew wider. Whatever happened now, whatever C. Todd did to retaliate, there was one inescapable fact. "I'm free!"

Now that she was rid of her job, Annie found something new to worry about. Jamie's fantasy.

"I never should've said I would do this," she said for the fifteenth time. But at least she was getting out of town, away from the clutches of *Undercover USA* for as long as the fantasy lasted.

Jamie's instructions were very sketchy, and Annie found herself wondering if she'd missed something somewhere. She managed to catch Jamie on her way out of the hotel, flying off to parts unknown to take care of the final details.

"Wait! Shouldn't I be coming with you, to get to the country house? And shouldn't my costume have arrived by now?"

"No, no," Jamie returned hurriedly. "I'm sending a car for you later, to pick you up here at the hotel. You're the special guest, dear, so you need to arrive separately."

"Well, okay, but what do I wear? What do I bring with me?"

"It doesn't matter." Jamie was already headed out the door. "Wear whatever you want to."

"But what about the costume?"

"All that's taken care of. The car will pick you up at ten-thirty, okay? And it will take you to the next stop, a little town not far from Angers, where I'll have someone to meet you and take you through the next stage."

"The next stage? What does that mean? Where is

Angers, anyway?'' she demanded. But she wasn't destined to get any answers.

"Don't worry—you'll love it!" Jamie called out. And then she was gone.

There was no mention of what Annie should bring or not bring, or even how long this blasted fantasy was supposed to last. How could she pack on incomplete information like that?

After parading through every store on the Left Bank with Jamie, Annie had seen enough clothing to rest assured that costumes for her and a cast of thousands would be provided once she got to wherever she was going. But surely she'd need her toothbrush and her blow dryer, plus several changes of clothes, to get her through the time before and after Jamie's elaborate costume ball.

Wouldn't she? Or maybe the costume ball was all there was.

"Maybe I'm going to be Cinderella, and throw a shoe at midnight," she muttered.

But if that was Jamie's fantasy, then what was all the secrecy for? There was no need to rent a whole house out in the country, not to mention digging up just the right seventeenth-century corset, for one simple Cinderella's ball.

In the end, she threw a mix of things into a bag, put on jeans with a crisp white blouse and a navy jacket, and hopped into the car Jamie had sent, feeling very unprepared for what lay ahead.

It didn't help her confused state of mind that she had no idea where the town of Angers was, or how long it would take to get there. Before long, her stomach was growling ominously, and she wished she'd thought to pack a lunch for what was turning out to be a trip deep into the countryside.

She'd hoped to get time to explore Paris, but all she was doing on her trip to France was sitting behind a series of windows, watching the country go by.

Thankfully the scenery was very pretty, very restful, and she began to relax. She even nodded off for a while, although hunger pangs woke her up before too long.

"Mademoiselle, nous sommes ici," the driver said loudly. As he opened her door with a snappy bow, he repeated, very slowly, "We are here, mademoiselle."

He'd pulled up in front of a modest country inn, a one-and-a-half-story gray stone building with a rickety sign creaking in the breeze. She couldn't read the faded letters on the sign, but she could make out a picture of a skinny rooster. The road, and the inn, appeared to be deserted.

"Mademoiselle," he prompted, offering her a hand. "You wish to come out now, yes?"

"Okay," she said hesitantly, slowly climbing out of the car. "But are you sure this is the right place?"

"Oui," he said smartly.

He removed her bag from the car, leading the way to the small, wooden door at the front of the inn. When he held the door open, she had no choice but to go in. She wasn't sure what would greet her, but she had the craziest feeling it was going to be scary. Would she see pirates, right out of *Treasure Island*? Or maybe a couple of musketeers, swilling beer and pinching the ample behinds of the serving wenches?

"What is wrong with me?" she murmured. "This may be a small establishment, and it may be in the middle of nowhere, but as far as I know, I'm still in the twentieth century."

Taking a deep breath, Annie put one foot through the door. "See?" she chided herself. "I told you it would be normal."

It was dark inside, with scarred wooden tables and chairs scattered around the middle of the room, a long bar with lots of bottles behind it, and even a few booths around the edges. In other words, it was exactly like hundreds of taprooms and taverns the world over.

At the moment, it was also empty. "Hello?" she called out, taking a few more steps into the room. She turned back in the other direction, planning to once more ask the driver of her car if he was absolutely sure this was the right meeting place.

But he was no longer behind her. Annie raced back to the door, rushing outside to scan the road for signs of the driver. But he was gone, and so was the car.

Meanwhile, her stomach growled even louder. "Oh, please!" she muttered. "I've been abandoned, I don't speak French, and I have no idea where I am or what I'm supposed to be doing. The last thing I need to worry about is hunger pangs the size of the Grand Canyon!"

The front door creaked open behind her.

Annie whirled, catching a pretty young girl peeking out the crack in the door. She didn't know whether to be relieved that there was actually a person there, or scared witless that someone had appeared out of nowhere. It didn't help her feeling of being in a time warp that the girl in the door was wearing a white mobcap and a long homespun dress with an apron over it. In other words, she looked like Little Miss Muffet, or perhaps just a waitress at Ye Olde Taverne.

"Mademoiselle Shona-boo-ro?" the girl asked timidly.

"Excuse me?"

"Shona-boo-ro?" she repeated carefully.

"I guess so." It might not be exactly "Jonesborough," but it sounded vaguely familiar. In the absence of a better option, she was willing to be Shona-whatever.

"Shona-boo-ro?"

"Yes, okay?" Still no reaction. More loudly, she said, *"Oui."*

It was the magic word. *"Bon."* The girl reached out,

grabbing Annie by the arm and hauling her into the dim recesses of the inn.

"Wait a minute," Annie protested, but her young companion was stronger than she looked. Before she knew it, they were halfway up a set of wooden stairs at the back of the taproom, headed for the second floor. "Where are we going?"

But Miss Muffet just smiled and shook her head, giving Annie a very charming I-don't-understand-a-word-you're-saying shrug as she continued to climb the stairs. Dragging Annie along behind her, she trooped down a low hallway, and then into a small, sparsely furnished room.

Sure enough, the hoop and the corset, plus the pieces of a full-skirted fancy dress, were all laid out nicely on the tiny bed that stood against one wall. For the first time, Annie began to believe she'd been brought to the right place.

"Oh, I see," she said out loud. "This is where I'm supposed to get dressed. Great. I can handle that."

In fact, she was fascinated. The clothes lying on the bed created an ensemble fit for Cinderella, even if her silent young companion was no match for the Fairy Godmother.

"Oh, well, I suppose Jamie technically qualifies as the Fairy Godmother," she murmured, fingering the beautiful blue brocaded silk of the skirt and dainty rosettes and ribbons that spilled down the front. There was a taffeta underskirt in a paler blue, and a separate bodice with a low décolletage, dripping in lavish lace.

It was fabulous, the kind of thing that belonged in a museum. "Wow," she whispered, wondering how in the world this elaborate outfit was going to work on her twentieth-century body.

Meanwhile, the girl slipped up behind her, and she began to tug rather vigorously at the sleeve of Annie's jacket.

"Yes? What is it?" she asked, but the maid just kept pulling. After a tug-of-war that lasted for several awkward moments, Annie began to get the idea. "Are you trying to take my jacket?" she asked.

No answer. Shrugging, Annie slid her arms out of the garment and handed it over, which got a big smile and a curtsy out of the girl. Miss Muffet spirited it away, hanging it over the back of a nearby chair, and then racing right back. Now, as Annie backed away toward the door, the girl had her grabby little hands out again, evidencing every intention of going for Annie's blouse.

"I can undress myself," Annie protested, warding off the girl and pointing at the door at the same time. "In private," she added, searching her brain for some French word that would vaguely fit the situation. "You may go now. *Allez*, okay?"

"*Allez?*"

"Yes, yes. You. *Allez*. Go away!"

"Oui, mademoiselle," she said, with a very hurt expression, making Annie feel like she'd committed a terrible faux pas. It was all Jamie's fault, for hiring someone to undress her in the first place. How embarrassing. Could Annie help it if she was shy about surrendering her blouse to strangers?

Little Miss Muffet limped toward the door, still wearing a woebegone expression, and Annie tried to think up a way to make her little helper feel better. Her stomach grumbled again, giving her an idea.

"*Je suis . . .*" What was the world for "hungry"? She knew it was somewhere in the first few pages of her handy phrase book, and she scrambled to find it in her purse. Thank goodness. There it was. "*J'ai faim,*" she said triumphantly.

She also found "Can I have . . . ?" so she tried that, too. "*Puis-je avoir . . . ?*" But there was no word for lunch, or dinner, or even food.

With a frown, she flipped the pages until she found

a few things that were at least in the right area. Besides, she knew how to pronounce them. *"Salades? Omelettes? Hor d'oeuvres? Soupes?"* And here was an especially good one. "Picnic," she said happily. *"Pique-nique."*

Before she knew it, the French girl was bobbing and smiling and making for the door, offering a stream of words that Annie could only hope related to bringing back big platters of food on the double.

With a sigh of relief, Annie shut the door securely, and then she stripped out of her jeans and her blouse as quickly as she could manage, intending to get the fancy dress completely onto her body before the maid came back.

Wasting precious moments, she gazed down at the things on the bed, noting that everything seemed to be complete. Except for the fact that there were no panties, no pantaloons, no knickers, no . . . anything.

"Those old girls didn't wear underpants, huh?" she surmised. "That's pretty scandalous."

Well, she was all for historical accuracy, but she had her limits. Wearing her own panties, she slipped on a pair of rose-colored silk stockings, and then wrestled into several petticoats, with the hoop skirt tied over that. So far, so good. But that left the corset.

Annie picked the thing up and regarded it dubiously. "There is simply no way," she muttered, turning it back and forth. Instead, she slipped on the boned bodice of the dress, fulling intending to wear it by itself. Unfortunately, it fastened in the back, so she couldn't hook it by herself, and its wide neckline made wearing a bra impossible.

As she was considering what to do about this dilemma, the maid returned. The young woman propped open the door, sliding in with a big tray, heaped with bread and cheese and fruit.

Annie could've kissed her. *"Merci,"* she said gratefully, rolling over in her hoop to help with the tray, planning to hold up her bodice with one hand and eat with the other. There was a chair, and she considered sitting down to eat, but the hoop made such niceties difficult at best. So there she stood, hovering over the food, nibbling bits of this and that until her hunger was at least partially assuaged.

Behind her, the girl clucked her tongue ominously.

"What?" Annie asked, nabbing a nice wedge of cheese.

But her pal didn't respond, just got to work undoing the ribbons on the hoop, pulling off the petticoats, and then rearranging everything Annie was already wearing, to put the petticoats over the hoop. She exclaimed something, apparently noticing for the first time that Annie had forgone the corset.

After what sounded like a "humph," Miss Muffet marched over and got the awful thing, carrying it back toward Annie like a shield. With a resolute expression, she pulled Annie away from the food and railed at her in rapid French, pointing back and forth between the food and the corset.

"I suppose you're telling me it's not going to fit if I eat anymore," Annie guessed. Defiantly she snatched up one last slice of apple. "I'm not going to wear that thing," she protested, but her words fell on deaf ears.

Mumbling in French, the girl spun her around, and then wrapped the corset around her in one fell swoop, sliding it under the top half of the dress and cinching it in the back until Annie couldn't breathe.

"Not so tight," she demanded, but the maid kept lacing, kept pulling, until Annie felt her ribs compress, and her rather modest bosom start to overflow the top of the horrible contraption. At the point where they truly were going to tumble right out, the maid finally stopped lacing.

"Jamie, I'm going to kill you," Annie swore.

She stood there, gasping for breath, while the girl plastered the bodice down over the corset, and then made another trip to the bounty on the bed, this time returning with the taffeta skirt, which she tossed on over Annie's head.

Deep breaths were impossible, and Annie began to see stars. "How did they survive, trussed up like this?"

Meanwhile, she was spun around again, fastened into the brocade overskirt, and then fussed over for about ten minutes, until Miss Muffet was satisfied that every flounce and every ribbon was in the proper place.

"I have never been so humiliated in my life," Annie told her, but her dresser just smiled.

"Oui, mademoiselle," she said happily. *"Magnifique."*

After which Annie got slippers, a tiny string of pearls, and an unceremonious shove into the chair, hoops flying, for a session with a curling iron.

"This is ridiculous," she fumed. "I feel like a mannequin, like no one cares that I have feelings and needs! That damn corset, these crazy clothes, and now my hair! I am going to kill her."

Or at the very least she was going to give Marie-Ange an earful, detailing just how horrible this fantasy was. "Maybe that's the fantasy," she grumbled, searching the room for hints of video cameras or two-way mirrors. "Maybe they think it's funny to torture me this way, while they all watch."

But her eager little helper just kept smiling, and soon Annie's hair was bouncing around her face in perfect ringlets. The back was pulled into a neat knot, and secured with more pearls.

"Très belle," the girl assured her, offering a hand mirror.

It did look pretty, and even sort of seductive, as if she had just fallen out of a road company of *Dangerous Liaisons*. But it was so uncomfortable. And so bizarre, not only to look into a mirror and see a perfect stranger reflected back at her, but also to glance down at her chest and see this bounty of cleavage.

She hoped the Prince Charming in this fantasy, the Duke of Whatever, was very nearsighted, or very shy. Or maybe he'd gallantly offer her his handkerchief to surreptitiously drape across the wide open space of her bodice.

"Voilà!" her maid said with a flourish, dotting a small black beauty patch on Annie's cheek and backing away for the total view.

"Now what?" Annie asked, rising unsteadily from the chair. She eyed the food tray with a certain yearning, but she knew even one morsel would be too much if she had to stay imprisoned in this dress. "I just hope Jamie's costume ball is over quickly."

At least she didn't have to wait long for the next phase of this spectacle to unfold. Her maid led her back down the stairs, to the front door, where she was surprised to note that the sun was already dipping toward late afternoon. Where had the time flown?

But there was no opportunity to worry about that. She hadn't been at the door more than a second or two when a coach drove up—an honest-to-goodness carriage, complete with a pair of white horses and a driver in an old-fashioned coat and breeches.

She'd seen something like this once before, for a royal wedding, when some princess or other got herded through London in a glass coach. This one wasn't glass, but it certainly was pretty, with a crest on the door, and a liveried footman waiting to help her. She hadn't realized such things existed outside royalty. Except for fairy tales, of course.

"It probably started out this morning as a pumpkin and a couple of mice," she whispered as the footman handed her up into the carriage. Somebody had undoubtedly waved a magic wand and turned the pumpkin into a coach, just like in the books. "I guess that means

I have until midnight until I turn back into plain old Annie.''

But it didn't take nearly that long for the fantasy to turn into reality, and to lose a bit of its sparkle in the process. Yes, the coach was beautiful. Yes, she felt like Cinderella. But every time they hit a tiny rut, she jolted up and down on the cushioned bench, giving her bottom a wallop, and almost knocking her off the seat a couple of times. Heavens! It felt like she was being dragged behind a runway horse.

All in all, Annie began to understand what the concept of progress meant. Horse-drawn carriages might be pretty and romantic, but luxury automobiles were a whole lot more comfortable. She decided she would take a block-long Cadillac limousine any day.

But they galloped along whether she liked it or not, while she bounced up and down back in the coach, until their speed suddenly dropped dramatically. The window on the door was very small, but Annie peeked out, overcome with curiosity.

"Holy smokes!" she said out loud. She was on a long, tree-lined drive, leading up to a huge castle. A real *castle*.

The closer they got, the wider Annie's eyes became. Jamie had said she was renting a country house, but this was no mere country house. This was a vast palace, a whirlwind of towers and turrets, with a wide stone staircase flanking the front, and a reflecting pool the size of a football field opposite the entrance.

A gaggle of people huddled on the stairs, with ten or twelve women in elaborate costumes like her own, and maybe fifteen men, all dressed like the Dutch Masters on the old cigar box. She had to shake her head to remind herself that she hadn't fallen into a time tunnel, that this was all make-believe, sprung from Jamesina MacDougal's fertile brain.

The people on the stairs turned to watch as her carriage approached, and Annie felt butterflies in her stom-

ach, as if she were just about to make her stage debut.
There was nothing to be nervous about, of course, nothing except the fear of falling headlong into the dust on
her way out of the carriage, or tripping on the stairs in
the unfamiliar long skirts. Either way, she'd be hoops-
up, showing off her underwear to all and sundry.
Charming.

The coach pulled to a stop, and her grip tightened
on the armrest. Why did I say I would do this? She
wanted her jeans back. She wanted her own century
back.

But the door swung open, and she knew she had
to come out. Annie took a shallow, unsteady breath,
accepting the footman's arm as she descended from the
carriage as slowly and gracefully as she could manage.
So far, so good.

The crowd parted, creating a path to the top of the
stairs, and she followed their lead, assuming they knew
what they were doing. As she lifted her skirts, carefully
taking one step at a time, she searched the faces, expecting to see Jamie there somewhere. Instead, she
found herself on the second step from the top, directly
in front of a bearded man wearing a small, round red
cap and a long clerical gown. He was holding a Bible.
A priest?

No, wait, she thought. I've seen someone dressed
like this before. In a movie, she realized. He was
dressed like the evil cardinal in *The Three Musketeers*
movie. But what was he doing here?

As she pondered the question, a different man moved
in next to her, edging over very close. This one was
in full Three Musketeers regalia, complete with cape,
sword, and a wide-brimmed, ostrich-plumed hat that he
doffed as he took her arm.

With the hat off, she recognized him immediately.
She just about fell backwards down the stairs, even as
she realized it all made perfect sense. Damn Jamesina

MacDougal, anyhow, for being a complete romantic and a complete ninny.

"Trevor," she said between clenched teeth. "What in God's name do you think you're doing here?"

"It appears I'm getting married," he said, raising one dark brow and offering his arm. "To you."

ELEVEN

"This can't be happening," she whispered, but no one paid her the slightest attention.

Trevor had a good grip on one side, and the crowd of onlookers pressed in from the other side, as the priest or cardinal or whatever he was mumbled some words over them, made the sign of the cross a few times, and then gave them each a ring.

"I can't do this!" she protested as Trevor shoved the ring on her finger. "Even if he is just an actor, and this is all a joke, it's sacrilegious. It's creepy."

"How do you think I feel?" Trevor returned sardonically. "I have to wear a cape."

"Yeah, well, you got a sword, too." She eyed the dashing, and very attractive, cut of his cavalier garments. He looked spectacular, the swine, from the heavy silver spurs on his boots to the dark breeches and short, fitted jacket, and the satin sash that sliced a dramatic line from his left hip to his right shoulder.

But it was the sword that really topped it off, although it was more like a rapier, very slim and long, sharp and lethal-looking. There was something about a man holding a weapon like that, something very elemental and overt, that simply blindsided her. Ignore it, she commanded herself. Concentrate on breathing.

That was no easy task, since her dress was so tight across the ribs. And if she tried to breathe more deeply, she risked overflowing her bodice altogether. She hadn't missed the fact that Trevor's eyes were glued to the rise and fall of her neckline. Perhaps he, too, was wondering if everything was going to stay put. Stay calm, she ordered. If she didn't want to panic, hyperventilate, and fall out of her dress, she had to get a grip on her emotions.

"Since you're holding cold steel, why don't you use it, and cut us a path out of here?" she asked pointedly.

"That wouldn't be sporting, would it?"

"I think it would be terrific."

But the priest cleared his throat loudly, glaring at Annie for talking out of turn. As she pressed her lips together, behaving like a good girl, the volume of his incantations increased. This part was Latin, she realized, although the syllables whirled around her like a windstorm, making her head spin. The ceremony seemed endless, almost as if it were real.

"Jamie's getting her money's worth out of this guy," she muttered, until he skewered her with his gaze again, and she shut up.

Then the cardinal looked right at Trevor, slowing stringing words together, but it sounded as if he was calling Trevor by another name. "Jean-Pierre Billaud, le Duc de Varenne," he repeated, and suddenly she knew what was happening.

The name was the same one Jamie had given when Annie asked her who the hero of the piece would be. But there was no real duke, even though Jamie had made it sound as if there was.

No, there was only Trevor, probably hoodwinked into agreeing to portray the handsome duke of Jamie's imagination, just as Annie had been conned into taking the role of the reluctant bride. Inside this bizarre fantasy world, they had reached the "Do you take this woman?" section, and the cardinal was waiting for Trevor's answer.

For one crazy moment, she thought he might say no. Trevor glanced down at her, flashed a hint of a smile, and then said, *"Oui."* And then he lifted her hand to his narrow lips, brushing a soft kiss across her fingertips.

Lord have mercy. Her heart lodged in her throat, and her eyes felt misty. Even though the ceremony was mostly in French, with the words garbled and strange, even though she knew this was all make-believe, at some level, she wanted to believe it. Every impulse she had told her to throw her arms around his neck and shout, "Yes! Yes! I do! I do!"

None of this is real, she repeated like a litany, as if the words would protect her. This is just Jamie's fantasy.

Clearly Trevor had no trouble keeping reality and fantasy apart. He was standing over there, looking cool as a cucumber, following along and nodding, even smiling down at her at what she assumed were appropriate moments in the ceremony. He was playing his part to the hilt, acting every bit the arrogant, high-handed duke who had stolen a bride from her native land and dragged her to the altar. She knew she was embroidering Jamie's tale, adding details she didn't have, but she certainly felt like a kidnapped, miserable bride. Well, she wasn't going to be miserable anymore. If this odd situation didn't bother Trevor, then it wasn't going to bother her, either.

When the cardinal fixed his beady eyes on her, calling her Anne Marie Catherine Sophie, princess of something or other that sounded vaguely German, she knew what she had to do. She threw back her shoulders, lifted her chin, and exerted firm control over her wayward emotions.

Do you take this man? Even though she didn't know

the words, she understood their meaning. The cardinal's question hung in the air.

"*Oui*," she tossed out carelessly, as if getting married to handsome strangers was something she did every day.

It's all a fake, she reminded herself. Too bad Trevor's hand, warm and strong around hers, felt so very real. She didn't have the will to take her hand away. In fact, she squeezed even tighter, borrowing a little of his composure, hoping it would seep through her hand and deep into her bones.

After the sun had set completely, leaving only a rosy glow on the horizon, the people in the crowd around them lit candles in the darkness. Another time, she might have found the flickering lights romantic. Now she was simply bewildered. It seemed like they'd been standing there on the steps of the château for hours, listening to the monotonous rumble of the fake clergyman's voice. Perhaps they had. Finally, blessedly, his words died out, and everyone around them began to cheer and shout and slap one another on the back.

They were all very good actors, these pretend-townspeople witnessing her wedding. They seemed genuinely happy to be participating. Maybe they were well paid.

They were also very boisterous. A little too boisterous.

"Trevor," she tried, but his hand was pulled away from hers, and they were both shoved inside the doors of the château, driven along by the raucous, energetic spectators behind them.

She was trying not to trip in her heavy skirts, trying to find Trevor somewhere in the uproar, but the crowd around her was pushing too hard. She had no choice but to run as she was herded into the hall, pounding her thin slippers on the hard stone floor of the entryway.

There was the priest again, blocking her path, holding out an official-looking document and a fountain pen that advertised Euro-Disney. Talk about anachronistic: That pen wouldn't come into vogue until the 1990s. He wouldn't let her pass until she took the pen, though, and the mob was pushing her from behind. And so, reluctantly, she accepted the pen and prepared to sign.

She couldn't be sure what she was signing, but she guessed it must be some sort of marriage certificate. Why it should be necessary for a sham wedding, she had no idea, but she scribbled her name across the bottom anyway, right under Trevor's. She noted, with a small smile, that he had also signed his real name, rather than his fantasy persona's. Like her, he probably didn't know what his character's whole name was.

Shrugging, she handed the certificate back to the priest, which action was accompanied by another round of high-spirited cheering. Perhaps she'd see the document again later, if, as she suspected, it was meant to be a souvenir she could take home from her little sojourn into the seventeenth century.

But she was quickly swept past the priest and on into the château. It was magnificent, with soaring, richly carved wooden beams, and huge tapestries, full of lords and ladies and unicorns, lining the walls. It was the sort of place one expected to see suits of armor, and sure enough, there they were. As a matter of fact, Annie almost collided with one on the mad dash through the castle.

They ended up in a long, dark dining hall, with an ornate gallery at one end. Several of the partygoers dashed for seats at the U-shaped table, as Annie looked around and tried to get her bearings. Like the rest of the castle, this hall was impressive, with a high, arched ceiling and clerestory windows. All it needed was King Arthur and a few knights, quaffing mead out of silver chalices, and maybe a minstrel strumming his lyre.

Quite a few more people had joined the celebration, including more dressed as nobles, and a big band of more simply attired folk, who must be acting as the peasant population. Whoever they were, they created a loud jumble of laughter and noise all around her. Annie now realized tonight's events were going to involve a meal, as elaborate platters and dishes began to be delivered around her. Was that really a peacock? Or something else decorated and stuffed to look like a peacock?

"King Arthur would never eat a peacock," Annie muttered to herself. But then she realized she wasn't even in the right country for him. "King Arthur is English, you dope, and I'm sure he's about five hundred years too early, anyway."

Oops. King Arthur was only a legend. Maybe Henry VIII was what she meant. Or Queen Elizabeth?

But it didn't matter. The medieval feeling was the same, even though Jamie probably would've pitched a fit to hear Annie merrily mixing historical periods. Where was Jamie, anyway? Shouldn't she be here, overseeing this chaos?

Annie glanced from face to face, trying to penetrate the costumes to find people she recognized. She knew that Kerenza wasn't among the guests; her shape would've been unmistakable, even in yards of fabric. But sure enough, there was Marie-Ange, skirting around the edges in an expansive emerald green satin dress with huge, poufy sleeves and a big lace collar that draped all the way from her chin to her shoulders. Lucky Marie-Ange. She got to be covered up. Although she didn't look all that happy about it. But then, Marie-Ange, with her perpetual anxious frown, never did seem happy about much.

And wasn't that Bertrand, the young assistant, radiating embarrassment as he hovered at Marie-Ange's elbow? Someone had given Bertrand a mustache and a tiny Vandyke beard to go with his jacket and breeches. He looked pretty goofy, but kind of cute.

Annie began to cheer up. This wasn't going to be so bad, if she wasn't the only normal person forced into a ridiculous outfit. The actors playing wedding guests were one thing; everybody knew that actors liked to dress up and make fools of themselves. But regular folks, like Marie-Ange and Bertrand, were in the same boat she was, feeling conspicuous and silly. And misery loved company, after all.

Still no sign of Jamie, though. Maybe she was up in the gallery, watching them all through a spy hole. Jamie would no doubt enjoy the adventure of that sort of devious trick, Annie thought grimly.

As she stood there, taking in the blur of faces and finery, someone nudged her elbow. She'd already been jostled quite a bit in the milling crowd, and she grabbed her arm away, ignoring the interruption. But then the nudge came again, harder this time. This was no mere bump in the crowd. Obviously someone was trying to get her attention.

"Trevor," she said with relief, turning toward the person who'd bumped her. She'd been wondering what happened to him. But it wasn't Trevor. "Jamie?" she asked, aghast. "At your own party, you made yourself a drudge? What are you, a waitress or something?"

"I'm a member of the duke's household—a serving maid, not a waitress," Jamie shot back. But her modest brown dress and apron were a disappointment, anyway, given all the fabulous fabrics and laces running around the banquet hall.

"Whatever you are, I am very angry with you," Annie began. She'd been bottling up a lot of negative feelings, all ready to unload on Jamie for getting her into this farce in the first place. "You lied to me."

"Not exactly—"

"For one thing," Annie interrupted, "you never warned me how uncomfortable it would be in this kind of outfit, with the corset and the low neckline and no underwear. It's horrible!"

Calmly Jamie announced, "It is completely historically accurate, you know, give or take a few decades. I tried for 1630 on everything, but the corset is probably about 1660, which required some modifications in the dress as well. But I did put it all as close in time as I could.''

''I don't care if it's from 2001,'' Annie returned. ''It's awful! Plus you promised me I would not see Trevor—''

''I never promised—''

''And you didn't say a word about a mock wedding ceremony, or any of the rest of this stuff. I'm still reeling!''

''I told you it was better if it was a surprise,'' Jamie said sweetly.

''Was it a surprise for Trevor, too? Or did he know what he was in for?''

''Well . . .'' Jamie colored slightly. ''He was rather more difficult to convince than you were, so I had to divulge a bit here and there. The costume, in particular, was a problem. But once I told him what I intended to do, and that you'd already agreed, well, he was unwilling to allow someone else to be the bridegroom.'' She patted Annie's cheek. ''Isn't it romantic? Unable to admit his feelings to you, but very fussy at the idea I might marry you off to someone else. Isn't that charming?''

''Good grief,'' Annie moaned. She needed to sit down.

As if reading her thoughts, Jamie said, ''Why don't you go and sit down now? You're at the head of the table, next to Tre— I mean, the duke. Where is he, anyway?'' She swore under her breath. ''Nothing is going properly.''

''It's not?'' Annie felt a prickle of unease. Unpleasant as this had been, she'd thought all the tumult was part of the plan. ''What do you mean? What's wrong?''

''It's getting rather out of hand in here, don't you think? All these people, the ones I hired to be the wedding guests—they're too loud and too frisky, and they're drinking themselves potty. It's like trying to control a room full of tipsy corgis.''

"What's a corgi?"

"A dog," Jamie said sharply. "A small and very yippy dog. Anyway, I don't blame them for being a bit obstreperous. That blathering priest went on forever, so they're undoubtedly all starving. Headed right for the wine, though, didn't they? I could throttle that priest. It's all his fault.''

"I did think he went on a bit long," Annie agreed.

"He isn't the one I thought I was getting," Jamie revealed. "The man I wanted played Cardinal Richelieu in the Comédie Française version of *The Three Muske-teers*, and was much grander, you know, with a voice like rolling thunder. Very impressive. This one," she said crossly, "was a last-minute substitution. Trust a real priest to put a damper on the proceedings, and not act nearly as much like a clergyman as a fake one.''

Not sure she'd heard right, Annie lifted a hand to her forehead, displacing a fringe of curls. "A real priest? Jamie, you didn't!"

"It isn't my fault," the romance novelist retorted. "The actor got sick, and the real duke recommended the village cleric as a decent substitute. Of course, the duke is also the one who found all these rowdy cele-brants, so there's more than a bit of blame to lay at his door.''

"Let me get this straight." Annie tried to take a deep breath to clear her head, but all she did was strain the seams of her bodice. "You got a real priest and real witnesses? All of these people think this is a real wedding?"

"Well," Jamie ventured casually, "it may be a real wedding.''

"What?" Annie choked. "Real? How?"

"I'm not sure." As she backed away, holding up her hands, Jamie's cheeks were as red as her hair. "I have to check. I mean, it *was* a real priest. Do you think that's enough to make it legal?''

''It better not be.'' Annie began to look around for pots or pans, anything she could use to smack Jamie over the head with.

''Why don't you ask Trevor?'' Jamie suggested helpfully. ''He's the lawyer.''

''Does he know about this? Are you two in cahoots?''

''Oh course not.'' Jamie managed a smile. ''But if you'd like to be the one to tell him, I wouldn't mind.''

''Jamie, I could honestly kill you,'' she bristled, advancing on the treacherous redhead, but Jamie scampered farther away, taking refuge between a couple of burly gentlemen who looked much more like gangsters than cavaliers, even with lace on their cuffs.

''Now, Annie,'' her friend soothed, ''you really ought to go and sit down. Relax. We can sort it all out later.''

''I'm not sitting down. I'm not relaxing,'' she vowed.

But Jamie whispered something in French to the two thugs standing next to her. They were smiling grimly as they bore down on Annie, one on each side. Without further ado, they lifted her by the elbows and started toting her over to the head of the table. All she could do was feebly kick her heels.

''Sorry,'' Jamie called out. ''I was hoping I wouldn't have to use them. But I had to have a backup plan, just in case you wouldn't go through with the wedding. It's all very much in keeping with the plot of my fantasy, of course. This is supposed to be an arranged marriage, and you're a very stubborn bride, you see, resisting to the end. It's much more exciting that way. You do see what I mean, don't you?''

''I see that you're absolutely out of your mind,'' she declared, as her guards dropped her unceremoniously at her place at the table and then stood there behind her, flanking her elbows. "Trevor is never going to let you get away with this. Trevor won't let you treat me like this."

If Jamie heard her, she gave no indication. "Blessings on the bride," she said loudly, which didn't sound French in the least.

To accommodate her skirt, Annie had to sit back a good twelve inches from the table, which made the idea of eating difficult. There was something that looked like roast chicken on her plate, as well as several other, fancier dishes she couldn't identify. The servants seemed to have given up on serving the meal in courses, as they were just bringing out piles of food willy-nilly now. Conspicuous consumption. But it all smelled great, and she might have actually eaten something if it hadn't been for her stupid dress.

She could get to her glass, however, if she leaned over just right and then held on to it. Silent, she sipped a bit of strong red wine, wondering when the champagne would enter the picture. She had no idea if the Framboise company even existed in Jamie's beloved 1630s, but she had no doubt the champagne of choice would show up somewhere on the menu.

Meanwhile, where was the groom?

There was a well-dressed man sitting one place over, and he tried to talk to her, filling her wineglass constantly, eagerly chatting at her in French. He was very deferential and kind, as if she really were the new lady of the manor, but she couldn't understand a word, and she couldn't think of anything to say to him, either.

How about "Can you call me a taxi, please?" or "Do you know where my groom has gotten to?" Where was her handy phrase book when she needed it? Finally he gave up his efforts to communicate, leaving Annie to her increasingly desperate thoughts.

The throng of guests was getting rowdier by the minute, chowing down on all the delicacies offered them, and tossing back enough wine to float the *Titanic*. As they offered toasts in her direction, Annie had time to worry about what the next step in Jamie's master plan would entail.

The hours were slipping by, and she knew it must be very late by now. She was so tired, so exhausted by all this turmoil, that it was difficult just to sit up straight. But her brain kept fastening on to one train of thought nonetheless.

They'd gotten married, now they were having a celebration feast . . . and then what? Maybe a wedding night?

"Don't panic," she whispered. "Maybe after dinner, all these drunk ruffians waddle out of here, and then Trevor and I take a nice, modern car back to civilization."

Or maybe not. Maybe . . .

She had a sudden vision of Trevor by candlelight, wearing nothing but his rapier. *You're my bride, and I mean to take my husbandly rights*, he would growl. She would cower in her nearly transparent nightie, trembling and afraid, until he pulled her down onto the Persian rug in front of the fire, and had his way with her.

"Oh, my God." She shot up in her seat, gulping down a whole mouthful of wine. "Don't panic. He wouldn't act like that, and you know it."

But she began to see the power in Jamie's fantasy, nonetheless. Heady stuff, this bartered bride/arranged marriage business.

"Maybe he's already escaped," she said hopefully. But he wouldn't do that, would he? Not without her.

Where was Trevor?

Just when she had begun to despair of ever seeing him again, he finally showed up. Thank God, he was wearing more than his sword. He'd shed his jacket and the rakish cape, but he looked as dashing as ever in a full-sleeved white linen shirt with black breeches that laced up the front. Like a pirate.

She now noticed, however, that he was also wearing a rather grim expression as he slid into the seat next to her.

All of the assembled guests, those dressed as peasants and nobility alike, made catcalls and various ribald noises as Trevor sat down. Annie winced. "Don't even tell me what they're saying," she told him. "I can guess."

"And you'd be right on target," he said tersely. "This is not exactly a classy bunch of people we have here."

"Trevor, where have you been? I've been going crazy."

He arched a dark eyebrow. "Why, Annie, this is the first time I can recall you actually being glad to see me. What's wrong with you?"

"I'm scared out of my mind." She lowered her voice. "Jamie has gone wacko with this fantasy of hers. The story goes that I'm here against my will, you know, the bartered bride thing, married to a duke, forced to stay in his castle. So she's got these guards posted behind me, just to keep me here. I feel like I'm in the Twilight Zone. Or maybe just inside the pages of one of Jamie's lamer books."

"I know." Very neatly, he began to cut up something on his plate that looked like a pastry in the shape of a bird. "I tried to figure a way we could get out of here, but she's got guards all over the place. So I guess we're staying. It's annoying, but hardly dangerous. What exactly are you afraid of?"

Well, that was the question of the hour, wasn't it? *If we're forced to spend the night together, all alone, in some achingly erotic set of circumstances, am I afraid that you'll ravish me? Or that I'll ravish you?*

"These peasant people," she said quickly, banishing any thought of Trevor and his damn sword. "They're all drunk and nasty. I'm afraid they may get ugly."

"They're already ugly," he countered. "Don't worry. The peasants don't revolt for another hundred and fifty years."

"That's comforting."

"Why aren't you eating anything?" he asked. "The food is a tad exotic, but it's really very good. Ahhh." He cast a wry glance at the stiff bodice of her dress. "Can't belly up to the table, huh?"

"Not exactly," she mumbled.

"Well, we can fix that. So," he said, proffering a morsel on the end of his fork as if it were quite natural to spoon-feed one's dinner companions. "Stuffed squab? Or would you prefer the tripe?"

She shuddered. "I don't know what either squab or tripe is, and I don't plan to find out."

"Look, you may as well eat while you can. Let's find something a little more mundane, shall we?" He speared a piece of chicken and brought it over close enough to taste, letting it hover there, tantalizing her nose. As she bit down, accepting his offering, he grinned unexpectedly. "Don't worry, Annie. We'll be fine. Once everybody in the hall falls down drunk, we'll retreat to our separate bedchambers, and then you'll get to say you spent the night in a real, live castle."

"Are you sure?"

He fed her another bite of chicken, and there was a spark of fire in his soft gray eyes. "Would I let anything happen to you?"

She hated it when he was being kind. She hated it that he was feeding her like a child, that he watched as each greedy little morsel slid slowly between her lips, that he knew and she knew they were both so turned on by this outrageous situation that they couldn't see straight.

"Looks like we get our wish," he commented. His gaze swept the room. "The guests are retreating."

Sure enough, most of the peasants were already straggling toward the doors. A few of the more nobly dressed celebrants remained, including Marie-Ange and Bertrand. And then there was Jamie, the simple serving maid, pulling all the strings from the sidelines.

A shout went up from one side of the assembly, and then they all started to chant along, raucously repeating the same words over and over again, swinging their glasses to the beat. Most of them were leering at Annie and Trevor as they yelled whatever it was they were yelling.

"What are they saying?" Annie demanded.

Trevor took a long swallow of wine. He sighed. And then he said, "Something on the order of 'To bed, to bed, they go.'"

"Oh, no."

"We don't have a choice, sweetheart. They're not going away until they think the duke has claimed his bride."

"Nobody's claiming anything," she assured him hotly.

"I know that, and you know that, but let's play along for now, just to get out of here, okay?" He shrugged. "They'll have to leave us alone sometime, and when they do, this whole nutty pretend wedding scheme will be over."

She thought about it for a moment, but she knew he was right. "Okay," she murmured.

"Good." He stood up from the table, giving her his hand. But when she took it, he swung her up into his arms, hoops and skirts and ruffles and all.

"Hurray!" the guests cried, or some French equivalent. And then they all crowded along behind as Trevor carried his bride up the stairs.

Up the stairs, Annie realized. *Up the stairs to bed.*

TWELVE

"Do you know where you're going?" she whispered, tickling his ear with her words.

"Vaguely." Trevor tightened his grip around her, hefting her and her bulky skirt in his arms, annoyed at himself for exactly how much he was enjoying the opportunity to press Annie up next to him this way. From his vantage point, he could see every precarious inch of her exposed bosom, count every agitated breath she took, watch every unsteady rise and fall of her breasts against the lacy edge of that damn revealing neckline.

It was intoxicating. It was maddening.

At the moment, he had every intention of taking her to her room, putting her down, and walking away, without ever touching so much as an inch of that beautiful little body. There was only one explanation for that kind of behavior. He had lost his mind.

Concentrating fiercely, he managed, "I am supposed to be the lord of the manor, after all. It wouldn't do for a duke to get lost in his own castle. So Jamie gave me a tour when I first got here, to allow me a certain familiarity with the terrain."

Darkly he added, "Given the twisted workings of

Jamie's mind, I wouldn't be a bit surprised if she hoped all along that I'd toss you over my shoulder and haul you away from the banquet to ravish you.''

"Trevor!" she protested. Her face flushed a rosy pink at the very idea of being ravished.

But he couldn't help himself. Some part of him really enjoyed baiting Annie. It was so easy to aggravate her, to tease her, to provoke a reaction.

Besides, carrying her like this, he could actually control her for a few minutes, even if he was having difficulty controlling himself. No matter how angry she was, she couldn't very well lash back at him while he swept down the halls of the Château de Varenne, keeping her safe from the mob of noisy miscreants who trailed behind them.

Gazing down at her pale, soft, delicious curves, he smiled to himself. Yes, he could definitely get used to this swashbuckling routine, and all its side benefits.

As he slowed in front of the door to her bedchamber, the crowd caught up to them, getting noisier and more obnoxious. They kept up the barrage of lewd jokes and provocative remarks, all the while beating spoons against wine bottles and clanging silver goblets against plates. It might or might not be historically accurate for the guests to serenade a seventeenth-century duke and his new bride in this obscene fashion, but Trevor was getting very tired of it.

"Your chamber awaits, my lady," he said sardonically, as he ignored the fray behind him and kicked open the door without further ado. After taking one step in, he whirled back. "Good night, all," he announced grimly. "The show's over." And then he used his elbow to slam the door closed, right in the eager faces of their pursuers.

"Trevor, put me down," Annie said plainly, wiggling in his embrace.

"When I'm ready," he said dangerously. He gave her a quelling stare, letting her feel the full brunt of his intensity, as he spun around, getting his first look at the bedchamber assigned to his reluctant young "bride." Although he wasn't absolutely sure what Jamie had had in mind with this sham wedding night, he had a pretty good idea of the kind of setting the loony romance novelist would choose for her royal seduction.

He wasn't disappointed. The room was small but beautifully appointed, from the pastel Aubusson rug near the hearth to the deep rose draperies around the four-poster bed. The faint scent of flowers permeated the room. He couldn't identify it, but it was lovely— vaguely spicy, just a little exotic, with a lush, heady undercurrent. Much like the woman in his arms.

"Gardenias," Annie whispered, as if she'd read his mind.

A cheerful blaze had been set in the marble-scrolled fireplace, providing the only light in the room. Its hazy reflection flickered against the silver champagne bucket and two slender crystal flutes that had been set on the bedside table.

All in all, a subtle but very romantic atmosphere. It promised pleasure, warmth, intimacy. In this room, in front of that fire, it was easy to imagine plying Annie with champagne and sweet words until she was dizzy with desire. And then he'd strip her out of her finery and make love to her for hours.

Just the thought of her slender, soft body wantonly entwined with his, with the flicker of firelight playing over her pale skin . . . It scorched him where he stood.

"Lovely," Annie murmured. She seemed pliant and soft all of a sudden, as if the room had worked its spell on her as well, and she leaned into him more closely, tracing a finger along the line of his jaw. "I didn't realize it would be like this."

His hot, dark gaze swept up and down her, taking in just what he was passing up. In that confection of silk and lace, she looked good enough to eat, with an impossibly tiny waist and high, full breasts. The slope of her neck, the curve of her shoulder, the soft pink lobe of her ear—he wanted to taste it all. Now.

He dropped her suddenly, setting her on her feet and stumbling away.

"Trevor, what is it?"

"The noise," he said roughly. "It's stopped. They've all gone away. Jamie told me she would dismiss everyone, even the servants, so that we could have the place to ourselves."

She licked her lip. "So we're all alone."

But his hand was already on the doorknob. There was no way he could stay there for one more second. Not if he intended to do as he'd promised, to leave her safe and sound—and alone—in her own bed tonight.

"I'll come for you in the morning," he muttered. "In the morning."

And then he strode out the door before he thought better of this idiotic impulse.

Annie was fit to be tied. Actually, she was fit to be *untied*.

She was exhausted beyond belief, anxious and stressed out, and still so overheated from the torchy way he'd looked at her that she couldn't see straight.

"It doesn't take much to get me stirred up, does it?" she asked herself. But her skin still felt prickly and hot, her knees were wobbly, and she couldn't seem to stop thinking about him and the room and the fire and what it could have been like. . . .

"All he does is look at me, and I'm a puddle on the floor. What would I have done if he'd actually touched me? I probably would've passed out at his feet, like some virgin on her wedding night."

Just like the bartered bride she was supposed to be. Good heavens! Jamie's fantasy was enough to drive a person stark, raving mad.

She groaned, pulling lamely at her corset. All she

wanted to do was get out of this horrible thing and go straight to bed, to throw herself under the covers and pretend that none of this had ever happened.

Unfortunately, that was impossible. After much wriggling and twisting, she had managed to get the top part of her dress off, every last tiny hook and eye, although she suspected she'd sprained something in the effort. The frilly layers of skirt were easier to deal with, and she disposed of them quickly, leaving all those ruffles and ribbons in a heap on the floor. Hoops and petticoats followed quickly.

But that still left the blasted corset.

"Why do these things lace in the back?" she lamented, stretching to reach a knot she couldn't see. "To keep the women helpless and dependent, if you ask me."

Well, she was good and helpless now. After pushing and poking and swearing at it, she came to the unhappy conclusion that she had two choices: She could either sleep in the hideously uncomfortable corset, or she could find someone to pry her out of it.

And she knew who that someone would be. The only trick was finding him.

He had been given a tour of the place, but she hadn't. So what was she supposed to do? Knock on every door in the castle?

She had no idea where the master's chambers would be located, and she didn't fancy dancing around the cavernous halls of the château wearing nothing but a corset while she conducted her room-to-room search.

"This is just an excuse," she berated herself as she hastily stepped back into the taffeta underskirt and shoved the silk bodice of the dress back on as well as she could. "You want to go and find him. You want him to peel off your clothes. It's what you've wanted all along. This is ridiculous, Annie. Ridiculous and very dangerous. You know what's going to happen if you find him."

Yes, she did. And she didn't care anymore. She'd had all she could take of this place and that man. She was sick to death of them. And sick to death of resisting.

As she contemplated beginning her search, she realized that she really ought to find something better to wear. But what? Her own clothes were still back at Little Miss Muffet's inn. Meanwhile, the top half of her body was a disaster. The unfastened bodice of the dress wasn't really covering anything, since it had been rather risqué to begin with, and now gaped open all down the back. Too bad. It was all she had.

Holding it up with one hand, she eased open her door and peeked out into the dark corridor.

Very scary. Nonetheless, she didn't plan to cower behind her door all night like a frightened child. Shoulders squared, she ventured outside.

Flickering torches lit the walls, and she crept along, calling out, "Trevor? Trevor? Where are you?" She passed room after room, traversing endless hallways, but everything was dark and silent. Surely there would be a light under his door. Surely there would be some way to know if she found the right room.

"Trevor?" she said again, trying to ignore the quaver in her voice.

And then someone grabbed her from behind.

Whirling, she jumped about a foot, dropping her hold on her top, letting it sag to her waist before she could catch it.

"Good God," Trevor said with feeling, staring at her almost completely exposed breasts.

Quickly she grabbed the bodice and yanked it up over the large bare spot. "What did you think you were doing, sneaking up on me like that?" she demanded, trying to get her breath to resume a more normal rhythm. It was no use. Inside that blasted corset, all she could do was gasp for air.

"What did you think *you* were doing, traipsing

around half-dressed in the middle of the night?'' He ran a shaky hand through his hair. ''Did I say half-dressed? How about *undressed*?''

''I'm dressed as well as I can be,'' she snapped back. ''That's why I came looking for you.'' With as much dignity as she could muster under the circumstances, she lifted her chin and faced him down, even though she was still shaking like a leaf. ''I discovered that I need help to get out of my costume.''

''You look like you did a pretty good job of getting out of most of it all by yourself,'' he returned harshly.

''Please, Trevor.'' She couldn't keep the weariness from her voice. ''Will you help me?''

There was a long, tense pause. He seemed furious with her, or perhaps furious with himself. His narrow, mocking lips were set in a hard, unforgiving line. Finally he said, ''I can't seem to turn you down, can I?''

His low, husky tone sent shivers down her spine. ''Thank you,'' she mumbled. ''Now, can you lead the way back to my room? I'm lost.''

That at least prompted a small smile. ''This way.'' He stalked ahead of her down the long corridor, not once looking back.

But Annie followed just the same.

Back inside the close quarters of her bedchamber, she tried to quiet the erratic beating of her heart. But there was no hope for it. Her pulse was racing like a runaway train.

She knew he was watching as she slipped off the wretched bodice again, letting it slide to the floor. But she kept her arms crossed over her chest, shifting around, giving him her back. And then she waited for him to make the first move, to release her from the prison of her corset. She could feel him back there, just behind her, breathing onto the top of her head. But he didn't touch her.

Trying to be patient, she felt each second tick by, until she thought she would lose her mind if this terrible silence continued any longer. She was petrified. She was on fire.

"Trevor," she ventured softly. "Could you . . . ? The laces are back there. I can't undo them myself."

Finally, blessedly, his cool, clever fingers skimmed the nape of her neck, dipping lower, finding the first string of the laces. Annie closed her eyes, fighting against the need to melt back into him.

"There," he whispered, loosening the knots, relaxing the top of the constricting corset.

Oddly enough, it only made it harder to catch her breath. It was as if the air in the small room was too heavy, too highly charged, to fill her lungs. She flared her nostrils, trying to gulp in more oxygen before she fainted, but it didn't help, not while his fingers continued their slow, tantalizing path down her back, slipping out one knot at a time.

"It was very tight, wasn't it?" he murmured, gently rubbing her skin with his thumb as he freed her from the last barrier, pulling out the last cord at the base of her spine. "I'm surprised you could breathe at all. Poor Annie."

"I, uh . . ." she began, but when his lips lowered to her neck, she forgot what she was going to say.

"Annie," he whispered, brushing his hot, wet mouth down her shoulder and then up to her ear. She felt more than heard her name on his lips. "Annie, I want you."

She dropped the corset.

From behind, his hands reached up to cup her breasts, to tease the hard, rosy nubs until she moaned with pleasure. She pressed against him, rubbing her bare back against the cool linen of his shirt, running her hands down his lean flanks to pull him even closer behind her, fitting herself to his thighs. The fabric of her petticoat was slick against his coarse breeches, but still she felt his arousal, and she knew for the first time how badly Trevor wanted her.

"Turn around," he urged. "I want to see you. I want to touch you. All of you."

Suddenly shy, she edged around to face him, trembling with nerves and need. But then he smiled at her, offering her a dazzling, incandescent smile, making her feel beautiful and desirable and cherished, all at the same moment. Her shyness vanished, and she was filled with the certainty that she was doing the right thing.

Was all of this happening because of a low-cut dress or a dashing rapier, or maybe because of the firelight or the delicate smell of gardenias? It was true enough that Jamie had created just the right atmosphere for sensual pleasures. But Annie knew in her heart that she was with Trevor, not simply because of the moment, but because of the passion and the heightened awareness that had existed between the two of them since the first moment they met.

It was inevitable. They belonged here together, as surely as night followed day.

Trevor framed her face with his strong, elegant hands, drawing her up to him, kissing her long and hard, deep and sweet, as if he couldn't get enough. Then, without breaking the kiss, he slid his hands into her hair, hurriedly pulling out the pins, scattering pearls everywhere as he pushed his fingers deep into the silky ringlets.

"It belongs down," he said firmly, running his fingers through the pale strands. He grinned again, lighting the darkness in his gray eyes. "It's impossible to pin down, just like you."

But she wanted to be kissed, not talked to. She rose up on tiptoe, fastening her mouth on his, hungrily tangling her arms around his neck. She splayed her hands inside his loose pirate's shirt, eager to feel his heartbeat, and the smooth expanse of his muscled chest under her fingers.

With a muttered oath, he broke away, shrugging out

of the shirt. And then they stood, skin to skin, exulting in the feel of each other, until, once more, he scooped her up into his arms.

But this time it was no mere ride down a busy street or even down a dark hallway. This time he set her in the center of the big old four-poster, swiftly stripping off his boots and his pants and then the vestiges of her clothes, as well.

He was stunningly beautiful. She'd always known it, ever since she saw that perfect face on the cover of her own paper, but she'd never realized how beautiful until this moment. He was all hard angles and lean lines, all darkness and elegance.

And then he slid in beside her.

Demanding and impatient, he was next to her, around her, with her, in a kaleidoscope of erotic images. She barely knew where one caress began and another ended, as Trevor touched her and kissed her. His lovemaking was as smooth and skillful, as brilliant and powerful, as everything else he did.

His mouth tugged at her breast while his fingers brushed the shimmering warmth between her thighs, and sensation spiraled through her. All she knew was the hot depth of her own desire.

She wanted him. She ached for him. She needed to feel him inside her. Now, before she died of wanting.

"Trevor," she murmured, tangling a leg around him, arching into him, lifting herself off the bed in her desperation to finish this madness. "Now, please."

"No," he breathed into her mouth. "Not yet."

"Yes. Now."

She reached for him, trying to pull him inside, but still he held back, stroking her, barely grazing her with his fingers, changing the rhythm each time she was almost there.

Higher and higher she climbed, but not quite high enough. As if he knew exactly what she needed, as if he were playing her like a finely tuned instrument, he denied her that final touch, that simple last nudge, to send her over the top. Shivering, trembling, furious, she could stand no more.

"Damn you," she moaned. "Now or never. I'll leave, I swear I will. I'll walk away and never come back."

He had the audacity to grin at her, and to make her wait a few seconds more. "The hell you will," he growled. He kissed her, full on the lips, and then, with a smile the devil could have called his own, he thrust deep inside.

"Trevor," she cried, shattering into fragments of pleasure so exquisite, she thought she saw stars.

But Trevor wasn't finished. Hard and deep, fast and furious, he took her higher still. And then he rolled onto his back, holding her securely, sliding her down on top of him, letting her set the pace. Her body had never felt so sensitized, so shaky, so easy to spark. As he stroked up into her, she held on tight, climbing the pinnacle again and again.

"Oh, Annie," he whispered. "God, you feel good."

Sweat-slick, sated, exhausted, she wanted more. She wanted him to lose control, to explode in a release as greedy as her own had been. "Come to me," she whispered. "Come to me."

She moved against him like a wanton, clenching around him, trying to make it so good, he wouldn't be able to hold back. But she surprised herself. As he cried out, surging up into her, she found herself once more soaring over the edge.

She had never known it could be like this. There weren't words to describe it.

"Bliss," she murmured, collapsing down onto his chest as his arms closed protectively around her. "This is what bliss feels like."

And then she nestled in next to him, feeling the gentle pressure of his hand smoothing the hair at her temple as she fell into the deepest sleep of her life.

* * *

She awoke to an empty room.

Annie sat up amid a tangle of bedclothes, confused and disoriented. Had last night been only a dream?

But no. For one thing, she was completely naked, and she hadn't gotten that way all by herself. She snatched an embroidered sheet up to cover herself while she tried to figure this out.

For another thing, the bed was an absolute wreck, with lacy white pillows on the floor and linens every which way, including upside down. There was no way she'd created that kind of disturbance with a chaste, innocent night spent sleeping alone.

"It wasn't a dream," she said slowly.

The final nail in her coffin was the sight of her corset, lying at the foot of the bed where she'd hastily abandoned it last night. Her body blushed with hot color just remembering the feel of his cool, clever fingers, sketching a trail of fire as they unhooked and untied her, all the way down.

"What have I done?" More to the point, what had Trevor done? Where was he?

Quickly she scrambled out of the bed and looked for something to wear, kicking aside all of last night's frippery. She knew she would never be able to see another Three Musketeers movie without melting into a puddle.

Finally she settled on wrapping herself in a sheet. She had to do something to get out this place, to find Trevor, to settle for herself exactly what had happened between them.

"I know what happened between us," she mumbled, forlornly slumping to a sitting position on the edge of the bed. She could remember every last detail with devastating clarity.

Annie took a deep breath. Oh, yes, she knew all the physical details. But what about the emotional side?

It felt to her as if something very important, something life-shattering, in fact, had occurred here. But was she only kidding herself?

The only person with answers was Trevor. And like the Casanova he was reputed to be, he had disappeared.

She heard a light knock on the door, and hope sprang up in her heat. "Trevor?"

"Non, mademoiselle." A middle-aged woman in a housekeeper's outfit poked her head around the door. "May I come in, miss? I bring the breakfast, yes?"

"Oh, breakfast. Wonderful," she said limply.

Actually, she *was* hungry. She hadn't eaten anything since the meager bread and cheese at the inn, unless you counted the few mouthfuls of chicken Trevor had so sweetly fed her by hand. But she wasn't going to think about naughty, seductive things like that, was she?

"Put the tray over here," she announced, moving aside the unused champagne bottle. Framboise would be unhappy to hear that their pretty pink wine had been completely forgotten in all the turmoil. Too bad. Sometimes life was intoxicating enough all by itself.

She glanced down at the croissants and hot chocolate she was being served, noting a folded newspaper on the tray, too. "What's that?"

"But you are famous, mademoiselle," the woman said with a smile. "My daughter, she loves these . . ." She paused, pursing her lips. *"Journal à sensation,* yes? Scandal sheet, is that what you call it? They have the *commérage,* the gossip, you understand?"

"It's a tabloid," Annie said, her heart sinking.

"Ah, *oui.* A tabloid, yes. So you are famous, you and the handsome monsieur. I thought it would amuse you to see it. Of course, it's very silly, but *amusant,* yes?"

"Amusing . . . yes," she whispered. She forced herself to pick it up, to take a good look at the cover without flinching.

Undercover USA. But what else had she expected?

Wendell had promised a good likeness, after all. There
she was in her leopard-print silk suit, laughing in Trev-
or's arms, with an unflattering photo of Princess Kerenza superimposed behind them, as if she were glaring
over their shoulders.

"Romance Contest Heats Up," it said. "Casanova
Case Carries Off the Prize as Kerenza Rages." Inside,
there was a longer story, implying that Trevor had
dumped Kerenza for some unnamed American, but that
maybe it was all a big double cross so he could win
the contest.

She swallowed. Trevor was undoubtedly furious. Of
course, it could have been worse. For one thing, there
was no mention of her name, her real job, or any hint
of orgies or sex scandals, the kind of thing she'd feared
they'd come up with.

On the other hand, the story and photos could have
never existed, too. And wouldn't that have been a much
better idea all around?

"Did Monsieur Case see this?" she said quietly. If
he had, it wasn't too hard to figure out why he'd left
her there without a word.

"But I don't know, mademoiselle. Would you like
me to ask him?"

Her head shot up in surprise. "Ask him? Is he still
here?"

"But of course." The matronly woman gave Annie
a beaming smile as she fished a small slip of paper out
of her uniform pocket. "He asked me to give you this
note, while he waits downstairs."

"Waits? But that means . . ." It meant he'd seen
the paper and was waiting to kill her with his bare
hands. Or maybe it meant he *hadn't* seen the paper,
and was waiting to shower her with morning-after love
and affection.

With trembling hands, Annie unfolded the message.
"You looked so beautiful in your sleep, I couldn't bear
to wake you," he'd scrawled. "Take a bath, clean up—

I had your bag sent over so you'll have something to change into—and then meet me downstairs. They've sent a car for us, but I'd rather take a walk on the grounds. We need to talk, don't you think?"

And at the end, he'd scribbled, "Love, Trevor."

Love? That wasn't what he would be feeling once he saw the front page of *Undercover USA*.

But maybe that's not what he meant now, either. After all, the note was sweet, even kind, but ambiguous. No great protestations of everlasting love, and no "thanks for the memory," either.

"Can you get my bag, please?" she asked the housekeeper, trying not to panic.

"Yes, mademoiselle. It's right outside."

"Thank you." As the woman got her suitcase, Annie made up her mind quickly. "Is there a back way out of the château?" she asked. "I need to get to the car without being seen. It's important."

The servant flashed her a very strange look, but she said, *"Oui, mademoiselle."*

As hurriedly as she could manage, Annie splashed some water on her face, tossed on yesterday's blouse and jeans, and sneaked down the back stairs. Taking a circuitous route around the outside of the rambling castle, she finally found her way to the front drive, where a car and driver waited.

"I need to go back to Paris right away," she told him. She jumped in the back and slammed the door, breathing a sigh of relief as soon as the startled driver pulled away from the Château de Varenne.

"It's better this way," she whispered. "I had the night of a lifetime, but it was only a fantasy, after all."

It might have been special and wonderful for her, but it was probably just business as usual, another notch in the bedpost, for Casanova Case.

"You don't believe that," she said flatly. In her heart, she didn't. But it didn't matter. Even if, by some remote chance, last night had meant something

THIRTEEN

"Listen, Jamie, I don't want to talk to you right now. I am still extremely angry with you," Annie said meaningfully.

She sidestepped the romance novelist, pretending to be caught up in arranging the pillows on the sleek sofa. This borrowed penthouse apartment—the setting for Annie's upcoming fantasy—was done up in stark black and gold, with strikingly modern furniture, gold star-and-moon pillows on the couch, and several large pieces of curvy Art Deco sculpture.

Bertrand, the assistant from Framboise, had found the place, and managed to borrow it from the owner, a company bigwig who was out of the country for several months. It couldn't have been more terrific, and there was really no need to fix it up. But Annie needed something to keep her occupied, and this was as good a ruse as any.

"So I indulged in a wee bit of matchmaking," Jamesina admitted as she tossed herself carelessly into a nearby sling chair. She was dressed in one of her flakier outfits, wearing a gauzy patchwork dress, ballet slippers, and a floppy hat with a huge red silk rose splashed across the brim. "You and I both know perfectly well that you and Trevor are mad for each other. It's not my fault if you keep finding fault with the poor man.''

Preferring not to discuss Trevor, Annie went back to the topic of Jamie's costume extravaganza. ''It was an unmitigated disaster, like everything else to do with this contest since I came to Paris.'' She gave Jamie a very black look. ''There is one good thing to come out of all of this, however. Since your fantasy turned out to be a nightmare, I ought to be a shoo-in to win the Romance Ambassador job.''

And I'm going to need it, she added silently. Heaven knows, nothing else in my life is working at the moment.

After all, she'd quit her job, she wasn't seeing Trevor, and the contest organizers were in an uproar over the tabloid article. Marie-Ange had hastened to assure her that no one blamed her, and for the moment, at least, Annie felt sure that no one had discovered the connection between her and *Undercover USA*.

But inside, Annie was miserable with guilt and embarrassment. She had lied about her identity, and she had aided and abetted C. Toad and his minions in their search for a scoop. Whether the others knew it or not, she was to blame.

It didn't help that Kerenza was on the warpath. Annie wasn't sure which bothered the princess more—the lousy picture, or the rumor getting out that Trevor had chosen another woman instead of her. The portly princess made no secret of the fact that she couldn't stand the sight of Annie, which made contest activities unpleasant at best.

And then there was Trevor. Annie had studiously avoided him, so she didn't actually know what his reaction was. *Coward*, she told herself again. Well, so be it. This way, he might be irritated for a few days, but he would soon go on to the next supermodel or actress, and his fling with Annie would become nothing more than an interesting memory. That, she thought, was just fine. Much better than him learning the whole truth, and hating her forever.

"So you think you're going to win?" Jamie inquired.

"I don't know about that, my dear."

"I have to win." With no Trevor and no job, her only hope was to get the Romance Ambassador position. If she lost it, too, she didn't know what she would do.

"I don't want to dash your hopes, but I refuse to believe that my fantasy failed," Jamie said cheerfully. "Marie-Ange loved it, and she's the one who'll decide whether it was a success or not."

"Marie-Ange didn't have to play the damn bride."

Jamie smiled mistily. "I'm sure she would've loved it even more if she had. Why, you should've seen the way she and Bertrand were looking at each other. My fantasy has sparked this lovely new affair, right under her nose."

"Marie-Ange and Bertrand, her assistant?" Annie gasped. "You're kidding."

"I'm perfectly serious. The atmosphere of my fantasy was very heady, and Marie-Ange and Bertrand simply succumbed."

"Good grief."

If Jamie was telling the truth, then Annie might as well kiss her last chance good-bye. She had to admit that all the outward trappings of the historical romance fantasy had been spectacular. Her own idea was rather simple, where two strangers found themselves trapped without power in a dark penthouse high above the city. How could it hope to compare with all that wretched excess of costumes and castles and peacocks on a plate?

Remembering the end result of Jamie's fabulous evening, with her and Trevor wrapped in each other's arms until the wee hours, Annie got even more depressed. If that wasn't romantic, what was?

"I don't know why I'm even bothering to try," she said gloomily.

"I'm surprised at you," Jamie remarked, propping her feet up on a cunning little footstool that was shaped like an elephant. "Cheer up. Your fantasy is going to be great fun. Who've you got lined up to play the strangers?"

"Nobody yet." She shrugged. "I haven't had a chance to think about it."

"You'd better get a rush on. There isn't much time left."

"I know, I know." She leaned back into the couch, staring at the ceiling. "I was thinking maybe the secretary at Framboise might like to do it. You know, ask a date . . ."

"Or you could do it yourself," Jamie suggested. "And then we could lure Trevor up here to play your mysterious stranger. It would be the perfect chance for the two of you to sort out whatever difficulty it is you're having."

"Don't be ridiculous," she declared, pounding one of the moon pillows right in the stuffing.

"He's obviously crazy about you, and you're throwing it away." Jamie shook her head, wiggling the fat rosette on her hat. "He's very upset, you know."

Upset because she'd ditched him for the second time? Or upset because he'd read between the lines of the tabloid article, and now he was ready to strangle her?

"I refuse to discuss this." She got up and paced over by the windows, gazing out at the rooftops of Paris. "I have a lot to do before everything is ready, and I'm not wasting my energy talking about something that is dead and buried."

"Well," Jamie ventured, obviously in the throes of some new idea, "if you're sure you don't want Trevor . . . perhaps you should try Marie-Ange and Bertrand as your strangers. They could use a push in the right direction, don't you think?"

"Jamie!" Annie protested. "Haven't you been listening to a word I said? You've got to stop this matchmaking stuff. Take it from me, it's no fun to be on the receiving end."

"Nonsense!"

"It's not nonsense," she stubbornly.

"Humph. Am I supposed to believe for one moment that you didn't enjoy yourself at the château, that you found all that time alone with Trevor distasteful?" The romance novelist, who was showing signs of being a bit too insightful, rose from her chair. "You haven't told me the details of what happened, Annie, dear, but I've a creative imagination. I would wager that you and Mr. Case had a simply ducky time."

"That's not exactly what I would call it."

"No?" Jamie crossed behind her, heading for the far wall.

"No!"

As she passed, Jamie said calmly, "All right then, I'll accept your story. You had a dreadful time, it wasn't romantic at all, and you don't care a fig for Trevor Case. Does that about wrap it up?"

"You don't have to be sarcastic."

"No, I'm completely serious." Jamie lifted her shoulders in an eloquent shrug. "You've convinced me."

Well, this sudden turn of events was certainly suspicious. "What are you up to?" Annie demanded.

"I thought I might ring up Marie-Ange, to see if she and Bertrand are available tonight to play out your fantasy." She smiled sweetly. "With your permission, of course."

The idea of Marie-Ange and her young assistant playing footsie with Annie's fantasy was a shade bizarre, but why argue about it? "Heaven knows I don't have anybody else," she muttered. "Oh, all right. Go ahead. Call Marie-Ange."

Annie watched closely as her least favorite matchmaker slipped over to the other side of the room and picked up the oversize receiver on the elaborate black and gold Empire phone. She heard Jamie say, "Marie-Ange? This is Jamesina MacDougal. As you're aware, Annie's fantasy is this evening. Well, Marie-Ange, with your help, it will be simply perfect. . . ."

Jamie turned around, balancing the receiver between her shoulder and her ear. She smiled broadly and gave Annie the thumbs-up sign. "Wonderful, wonderful . . . Listen, Marie-Ange, Annie is finishing up here at the apartment, so why don't I get the details from her, about the timing and so forth, and then I'll drop by your office and fill you in? Good, good."

She hung up the phone, and reported promptly, "All set."

"Okay," Annie returned doubtfully. "But why are you doing this?"

"Oh, you know me," Jamesina said gaily, throwing up her hands. "I love a good romance!"

"Right." Although she couldn't figure out why, Annie was feeling a tad leery of this scheme. Nonetheless, she went along. "Look, here are the details for Marie-Ange and Bertrand. I've arranged for the power to be shut off at midnight on the dot. Marie-Ange should be here a little before that, say, eleven forty-five, and Bertrand . . ."

This still seemed unbelievable. That sweet, shy boy and his *boss*? Even if the two were carrying on some hot and heavy affair, Bertrand was hardly the fierce, dangerous stranger Annie had envisioned for her penthouse escapade.

Shaking her head, she continued, "Bertrand should plan to arrive just as the power goes out, so that they meet in the dark, you see? That's really all there is to it—I've arranged for food, mostly chocolate, and then there's tons of champagne, of course. I'll have candles in the apartment, but they'll have to find them. Whatever else they do is up to them." She glanced over at Jamie. "I guess that's it."

"And what do you have left to do?"

She fished in the pocket of her jeans for her list. "The food, the flowers, and the ice for the champagne. It's all ordered, but I have to pick it all up, and then set it out up here."

"When do you think you'll be done?"

Her eyes narrowed. "Why are you asking all these questions?"

But Jamie was all innocence. "You had such a terrible time at my fantasy, so I thought I'd try to make it up to you by being helpful."

That *did* sound reasonable, and Annie began to feel badly that she'd mistrusted Jamie, whose impulses were good, even if her methods were questionable.

"Okay," she said quietly. "I accept your help. Thank you."

"You're very welcome." Jamie made for the door, headlong into her mission to inform Marie-Ange, but she turned back at the last moment. "Oh, Annie, I've just had a thought. Since it promises to be a long evening, what do you say if you and I go out after you're done? You keep complaining that you haven't seen anything of Paris. Why not go out, just the two of us, to a discotheque? Perhaps some charming Frenchmen will ask us to dance." Slyly she added, "It's a dandy way to forget about Trevor."

"I've already forgotten about Trevor," Annie said testily.

"Then you'll come?"

"I guess so."

"Terrific!" Jamie swung open the door. "I'll come by for you here, all right? Just in case there're any last-minute tangles. What time do you think?"

"Ten," Annie decided. If she left at ten o'clock, the ice around the champagne might melt before the young lovers arrived, but that seemed a small price to pay to get out of this place and blow off some steam. Jamie's idea of a night on the town was starting to sound better and better.

"Ten it is. Oh, and Annie . . . wear something sensational." Jamie winked at her. "We have to impress those Frenchmen, after all."

"I'll see what I can do." She had this great hot pink number, a very short, sparkly silk T-shirt dress that she'd bought just for her trip to Paris and never worn.

Why not try it out? The dress wasn't going anywhere else, and neither was she.

Annie rearranged the pillows one last time. She wanted everything to be perfect, even if it was only Marie-Ange and Bertrand who'd get to try it out.

"Let's see," she mumbled, glancing at her watch as she hurried into the bedroom. "It's quarter to ten. I have just enough time to change my clothes and ice the champagne before Jamie gets here."

She stuffed her grubby work clothes into a small bag, and then grabbed the bright fuchsia dress off the hanger. Since she was trying to rush, she was hardly at her most coordinated, but she managed to get her stockings and the bugle-beaded dress on without running or ripping anything. The fact that she'd brought a garter belt instead of panty hose further complicated matters.

There was a mirror in the adjacent bathroom, and she quickly brushed her hair and applied a little eyeliner and mascara to spruce up her looks.

All in all, she looked pretty good, she decided, giving herself the once-over in the mirror. All she needed was . . .

"Shoes," she said out loud. Shoving one foot into a silver sequined high heel, she poked around on the floor next to the bed, searching unsuccessfully for the matching shoe.

"It can't have gone very far," she muttered. "I had them both when I dumped everything out of the bag."

With a muffled oath, she got down on her hands and knees to see if the darned thing had rolled under the bed. "Where are you?" she demanded, sticking her head under the side of the black satin bedspread, and reaching under as far as she could. She just had her finger on the heel of the shoe . . .

When the whole room went black.

"What?" She jumped, smacking her head on the underside of the bed frame. Why had everything gotten so dark all of a sudden? Had the bulb in the bedroom lamp burned out?

But when she scooted out from under the bed, still holding her wayward shoe, she realized that the darkness was too pervasive to be caused by one blown light bulb. And then it hit her, as if the puzzle pieces fell into place.

"The power went off," she whispered, peering down to read the numbers on her watch. "Two hours too early."

Well, at least she'd located her shoe before all the lights went out. Groping her way along, she made it out into the hallway, where the glow from the living room brightened the deep shadows. Thankfully she'd left the drapes pulled wide open to let in the shimmering skyline of Paris, and that furnished enough light to illuminate general shapes and distances, as long as she stayed near the windows.

Sighing with relief, she laid her forehead against the cool glass. Although the early power outage was inconvenient, it wasn't a disaster. After all, Jamie would be arriving in a few minutes, and they would still go out on the town. No one would even know that the apartment had been cloaked in darkness for an extra two hours. And when Marie-Ange got there, the fantasy would proceed as she scheduled.

So someone had screwed up and pulled the switch a little prematurely. No big deal.

Much encouraged, she felt her way to the kitchen, managing to locate the champagne bucket and the ice in the dark, and to put a couple of bottles in to chill. The exotic chocolates she'd bought were still in the fridge, although its cooling properties had clearly departed when the lights did.

Annie stood there, peering into the silent, dark refrigerator. She could just make out the outline of the specially designed white chocolate basket, filled with heaps of strawberries and raspberries, dipped in dark and milk chocolate. There were boxes of tiny chocolate champagne bottles and glasses, and another carton filled with miniature stars and moons of various sizes. Slamming the door closed, she could only hope it wouldn't melt into one big, indistinguishable lump of chocolate before the lucky couple got there.

Scrape. The front door to the apartment creaked open. Scuffle. There were footsteps in the living room.

"It's just Jamie," she murmured under her breath. "She got here, the lights were out, so she came on in to find me."

But then a deep, masculine voice called out, "Bertrand, is that you?" and she knew Jamie wasn't coming.

Trevor's tall, lean form appeared, silhouetted in the doorframe, and Annie could only sag back against the kitchen counter. He was wearing a dark suit and a very white shirt that glowed softly in the darkness.

"I've been set up again," she whispered. "I can't believe I fell for this."

"Annie?" He actually seemed surprised. "What are you doing here?"

"I might ask you the same thing."

The kitchen seemed very small, very dark, and very crowded at the moment. She wanted to shove past him, to get some breathing room in the living room, but that would've meant touching him, brushing against him. And she couldn't do it. She was too much of a coward.

"What is this?" he asked warily. "What kind of game are you playing?"

"I was expecting Jamie," she insisted. "We were supposed to go out, to a disco or something. But I guess Jamie—and you—couldn't resist playing me for a fool one more time."

"Be quiet, will you?"

He advanced on her, taking her shoulders in his hands, and she gasped, shocked at the impact of his touch. Her whole body stiffened, becoming instantly aware, instantly aroused.

"Whatever you think, I didn't come here to see you," he said tersely. "I don't fancy the idea of setting myself up for another one of your kiss-and-run games."

"I—" she protested, but he ignored her, running roughshod over her words.

"Like you," he said, "I've been played for a fool. Bertrand fed me some nonsense about hitting a snag in his relationship with Marie-Ange. He told me he needed some advice, and suggested that he and I take a night out, just the guys. He told me to meet him here at ten o'clock."

"But that's when Jamie was supposed to come for me."

Trevor stared down at her, as if he were judging for himself the sincerity of her words. His hands tightened briefly on her arms, but then he released her completely, backing off. "It appears that there was a conspiracy to put us together tonight. I wonder why."

"I understand Jamie getting in on it," Annie began. "She's got this neurotic obsession with turning us into the love match of the century. But Bertrand and Marie-Ange . . . Why would they do this?"

"Just crazy, I guess."

"They trapped me in my own fantasy," she whispered.

He turned away from her, fiddling with something on the counter, and Annie heard the harsh pop and swish of opening champagne. The sound was startling loud in the silent apartment. Without bothering to find a glass, Trevor raised the bottle to his mouth, knocking back a big swig.

She couldn't stay there, listening to those sounds, imagining his lips framing the bottle neck, and the bubbly wine sliding down. Shivering, crossing her arms over her chest, she rushed past Trevor and out of the tiny kitchen.

She huddled on the sofa, arms around her knees, doing her damnedest to pretend he wasn't there. Jamie and the others might've been able to trick them into sharing the same apartment for a few hours, but they couldn't force her to get anywhere near him.

But he followed her into the living room, still toting the champagne. "I don't suppose there's any way out of here," he asked grimly. He was very visible now, in the light streaming in from the window, as he set down the bottle and eased around to look at her. "Elevator? Stairs?"

Dully she responded, "There are no stairs, except to the roof. You can climb up there and try waving for a helicopter if you want to, but that's about it."

"Charming." As if he were preparing to work his way out with manual labor, he stripped off his jacket, loosened his tie, and rolled up the sleeves of his pristine shirt. In the fractured light, Annie's eyes followed every precise motion. "You'd better hope there's not a fire."

"I'm not planning on starting one," she retorted. "Are you?"

His voice was low and husky when he said, "I'm seriously thinking about it."

Oh, brother. She knew better than to play this kind of game with him. The embers inside her were ready to burst into flame, and he knew it.

"You can try the elevator if you want to," she said slowly, "but I'm guessing that it won't come back for you. My instructions were that all the power to the apartment, plus the phone and the elevator, were to be turned off, as soon as both people had arrived." She licked her lip, letting herself ramble on, even though she knew she was flirting with danger. "That's the fantasy, you see. Two strangers, trapped in a penthouse high above the city. All night they have nothing to do but discover each other."

"I think we're past the point of discovery, don't you?" The shadows slashed across his elegant features, giving his cheekbones and his jaw a murderously hard line. "If my memory serves, we went well past that point. Several times."

She flinched. He could be so cruel when he wanted to. With just a few well-chosen words, he'd managed to remind her of every single erotic moment of the night they'd spent together. It was torture. Annie tucked her head down onto her knees, pressing her lips together, determined not to rise to the bait.

"You're such a coward," he said in disgust. "I might've known you'd refuse to fight when the chips were down."

Her head snapped up. "I am not a coward. I just don't choose to get into a battle of insults with you. You win, okay? You're smarter and you argue better, and you have all the answers." She could feel her emotions running away with her, but she couldn't stop. "Can't you just leave me alone?"

"No," he said fiercely. He hauled her up off the couch, pulling her up until her face was only inches from his. "I can't leave you alone," he bit out. "I see you, and all I can think about is getting my hands on you."

FOURTEEN

"Trevor, you're scaring me," she whispered.

He dropped her suddenly, and she spilled back onto the couch. Stunned, she just sat there, watching him pace.

Swearing a blue streak, he shouted, "I am so angry, I'd like to punch something."

Annie was very confused. She'd figured he would be harboring a certain indignation, even a little hostility. But losing control like this, raging and cursing . . . it was so unlike the cool, collected man she knew. It was almost as if he were deeply, irrevocably wounded. But that wasn't possible, was it?

"I know that you must be very upset about the article in *Undercover USA*," she ventured, "and I'm very, very sorry about that. But, Trevor, I didn't know. I swear."

"Do you think I care about that stupid rag?" He raked a hand through his hair. "It's a minor annoyance at best. No, Annie, that has nothing to do with this. I thought you knew . . . Any moron should understand . . ."

"But I don't understand," she murmured.

"I am angry because you keep running away from

me," he growled. "You're driving me out of my mind."

Once again, he bridged the distance between them. But this time he joined her on the couch, gently nudging her around until she faced him. "I love you," he said roughly. "I love you."

She was absolutely stunned, frozen where she sat.

"Well, there you have it. It's out." His laugh was bitter and short. "Confessions are easier in the dark, I guess."

But she could still see every inch of his gorgeous, face, every line of tension. She could feel him next to her, his shoulder touching hers, his thigh brushing hers. *He said he loved me*. There was pressure on her chest and behind her eyelids, and she knew she couldn't speak.

"We do have a chance together," he went on. "But not if you can't trust me enough to fight it out, to tell me what's bothering you."

Staring straight ahead, vaguely registering that the sparkling lights of Paris were still shining out there, she couldn't seem to find words to respond. This was all so very unexpected. The idea that he might love her, might really and truly have those kinds of feelings for *her*, seemed impossible. And yet he'd said it. And Trevor was not a man who made things up on the spur of the moment.

"Annie," he said softly, "if you were disappointed, the night that we were together at the château, if it wasn't what you wanted, I need to know."

She almost choked. He was worried about *that*? "I wasn't disappointed," she managed. "Believe me, I wasn't disappointed at all."

"Then why did you run away? I thought everything was going great." He shook his head in consternation. "And then the next thing I know, you're gone, and I'm feeling like an idiot again."

"It wasn't anything to do with you," she told him quickly. "It was me. I just couldn't handle . . ."

I just couldn't handle not being good enough.

On the one hand, there was Trevor, so perfect, so wonderful, the answer to any woman's dreams. And on the other, there was Annie, the tabloid hack, who'd lied to him and deceived him from the moment she'd met him. How could this possibly work?

"Tell me the truth, Annie," he demanded. "All of it."

But she couldn't do it. "You don't know how ugly the truth is, or you wouldn't want to hear it," she whispered.

Silence hung between them for a long beat. "I know about Chessy, if that's what you mean."

"Chessy?" She shot him a mystified glance. "What about her?"

"That you lost custody of her to your jerk of an ex-husband."

She smiled at the idea that Trevor Case could sound so protective, so loyal. "You don't even know my ex-husband," she reminded him.

"I know he's a lawyer, and I know he put you through the wringer."

"Well, that much is true, anyway."

"Annie, look," he said softly, taking her hand and folding in between both of his. "I could help you get her back. It's just a legal wrangle, a case of who can hire the biggest gun. You don't know how good I am at what I do. If you want her back, I'll find a way."

He truly took her breath away. "I can't believe you would do this for me," she murmured.

"I've thought about you and me, and what the right course is for us. I've thought about it, long and hard." He smiled sardonically. "You gave me plenty of time to think, while you kept running away and leaving me stranded. At first, I admit, all I wanted was to find you and put you over my knee. But then I realized, this all stems from losing Chessy. You were unhappy, you weren't thinking straight, and you made some bad decisions.''

He'd lost her on that one. What bad decisions was he talking about? And what did that have to do with Chessy?

"I really appreciate how kind you're being," she said slowly, feeling her way through this conversational puzzle. "When I got divorced, and he took Chessy, I *was* really low. The worst part was that he only wanted her to spite me, and that we both knew she would've been happier staying with me." She hadn't thought about any of this for so long, and it felt strange to stir up old feelings. "But I'm still a little surprised that you would take Chessy so seriously."

Impatiently he returned, "Of course I take her seriously. How can you think I wouldn't?"

She gave him a very searching look. "Trevor, this is very sweet, but I don't really think I can blame my problems on losing my cat."

"Cat?"

"Chessy. My cat. You said you knew about my cat."

"Oh, my God." Trevor slumped on the sofa, lifting a hand to his forehead. "I thought she was your daughter."

"Well, she is, in a way, but not my human daughter." Annie laughed out loud. "That's what you thought?"

"Yes, that's what I thought," he mumbled.

"This is a riot. You think I'm some poor, distraught mom, denied custody of my baby. . . .''

But then the implications hit her. "Trevor," she blurted, "if you know about my divorce and Chessy, then . . ." Her reasoning might be a bit slow, but it came through eventually. Fearing the worst, she turned on him. "Then you know all of it, don't you?"

"About Annie Porter, you mean, ace correspondent for *Undercover USA*? Yeah, I know about that, too."

"Oh, my God." She felt like she'd been doused with a bucket of cold water. She had to think, to plan . . . but her brain had turned to oatmeal. "I didn't want you to find out. I never wanted you to find out! How long have you known?"

"Almost from the beginning."

"But you never said anything!" This was her worst nightmare, and he didn't even seem to care. He just sat there, talking in a monotone, as if it didn't matter that she'd sold her soul to *Undercover USA*. "You didn't rat on me, or yell at me, or anything," she told him, her voice rising. "You would've been perfectly justified if you'd exposed me to Marie-Ange and ruined my life, but you didn't!"

"I know."

She was so annoyed, she made a fist and belted him one of the shoulder. "Well, why not?"

His response was a lazy, crooked smile.

"Well?" she persisted. "Why didn't you turn me in?"

His soft gaze held her and warmed her. "Because I liked you," he said simply.

The man was positively infuriating. He kept taking all of her assumptions and turning them upside down. First he claimed he loved her. And then he said he knew about her trashy job and he didn't care! How could this be?

"And do you still *like* me," she asked sharply, "now that you know I didn't fall headlong into the sleazy world of tabloids because of some deep emotional scar over my cat?"

"God help me," he said, sighing deeply. "Yes, I do."

How could she *not* be head over heels in love with this man? Now, if only she felt as if she deserved him.

"I want you to know that I didn't do anything shady

or underhanded once I entered the contest." It had become important that she explain a few details, and she leaned across him, taking him by the shirt collar. "I really wanted to win so that I could get the Romance Ambassador job and leave *Undercover USA* forever. I wanted to be proud of what I did for a living, not dreading going to work every day."

"It's okay, darling. I understand."

But she kept explaining anyway, scooting over closer until she was practically in his lap. Her shoes fell off, and her dress was riding up over her thighs, but she had no time for that now. "Trevor," she said urgently, "the article that appeared in the paper had nothing to do with me. I swear I didn't take one picture or write one word about you."

He raised a dark eyebrow. "You tried, though."

"On the yacht . . ." Annie had the grace to blush, remembering the convenient way her camera had gone careening into the sea. "You did it on purpose."

He nodded.

"I couldn't do it, though," she told him. "Even then. It's hard to explain, but I just couldn't do it anymore. And then, finally, I knew that even if I didn't win the contest, or get to be the Framboise Ambassador, I had to quit."

"You quit? When?" he asked, pulling her all the way across his lap.

"When?" She was having trouble concentrating in this position, with his fingers sliding around the beaded hem of her dress, inching the fabric even farther up her thigh. "The morning before I left for the château. The morning before we . . ."

"Made love," he finished for her, breathing the words into her ear, nipping gently at her neck, shifting her more securely into his lap so that she straddled his thighs.

"I want you to know," she said shakily, "what happened. . . . It was really special to me. I didn't leave because I was disappointed or because anything was wrong with . . ."

His hand ventured under her hem, sketching a path of fire across the top of her stocking, teasing the nub of her garter, dancing closer and closer to the edge of her panties.

"Ohhh," she breathed. As his fingers kept up their crazy game of hide-and-seek, he was nibbling her ear and the tender slope of her neck, and all she could do was arch into him, wobbling there in his lap like a rag doll. "Let me finish," she said hoarsely. If she didn't get everything she had to say out within the next thirty seconds, she knew her mouth would be too busy for words. "About that night, at the château . . ."

"Make it quick," he demanded, sliding his hands completely under the dress, cupping her round bottom, nestling her tighter against him.

"It was so wonderful between us," she managed to say. Her words tumbled out, one after the other, rising and falling with the motion of his clever hands. "But I was scared. I didn't know how you felt. In the morning, you were gone and I was scared. And then I saw that horrible newspaper, and I thought for sure you would figure out that I was involved."

He popped one garter, and then another, and she went stock-still in his arms, afraid that the pressure building inside her would only get worse if she moved.

She swallowed, trying very hard to say what she had to say. "Trevor," she said, breathing raggedly, "you are a very overpowering man. You are so smart and so successful, and I can't compete with that."

"I'm not asking you to," he murmured, kissing her full on the lips.

"But *I* am." She tore her mouth away from that devastating kiss, and slammed her hands down on top of his, pushing them back to less dangerous turf. "I want you to look at me and respect me, Trevor, the way that I respect you. I knew that if I told you where

I worked, you would look at me and see an unethical, immoral hack who lies for a living." Now, gazing into his gray eyes, she saw the hot flicker of desire, but not what she craved. "I couldn't bear it," she whispered.

"Annie, I love you," Trevor said quietly. He dusted a soft kiss into the curve of her neck. "I respect you." Another kiss followed, this one brushed lightly across her collarbone, where her neckline lay. "And I trust you."

"How can you possibly—" she began, but he cut her off, placing a finger across her lips to keep her quiet.

"When we stole my essay from Framboise, you knew immediately I didn't write it. But you never told anyone. Why?"

"I wouldn't do that," she protested.

"Exactly." His lips curved into a wicked smile as he kissed her again, longer and deeper this time. "I promise," he said, breathing the words into her mouth, "to respect you and to trust you, and to love you within an inch of your life, as long as you promise never to run away from me *ever* again. Is it a deal?"

"Okay."

"Thank God." He tipped her back into the couch, scattering little moon and star pillows every which way, pulling her down underneath him. Her dress slid above her hips in the process, which elicited a knowing grin and a roving hand from him immediately.

"As long as we're making promises," Annie stalled, catching his fingers and clasping them in hers, "I think you should promise to give up all of your clients who are fashion models or actresses or anybody else who is certifiably gorgeous."

He frowned down at her. "So you don't trust me?"

"I trust you," she hastened to assure him. "I just don't trust them."

He grinned. "If you want it that way, Annie, consider it done."

"And will you really help me get Chessy back?"

"Done."

"And will you swear never to ask me to participate in any event which requires clothing older than 1970?"

"I don't think I can promise that." His eyes sparkled with all sorts of mischief. "I developed a real fondness for that corset."

There was a long pause as she gazed up him, drinking in every inch of the man she'd won. It didn't seem fair, but who was she to fight destiny?

In what she tried to make a low, sexy voice, she murmured, "I'm willing to negotiate."

"Even if it takes all night?"

Annie smiled. "Definitely."

"We both know Jamie's going to win," Annie said under her breath. "I don't know why we even bothered to come."

"We don't know anything."

"Oh, pooh. Jamie's going to win, the press is going to be there in droves—probably including C. Todd Entwhistle himself—and we're both going to be miserable." She tucked her arm securely through his as he led the way to the last Framboise press conference. Grimly she warned, "You don't know what you're in for from the Toad and the other people I used to associate with."

Trevor dotted a kiss on the top of her pretty blond head. "And you don't know what you're in for from the people I used to associate with."

She shot him a curious glance. "Like who?"

"Like Zoë and Veronica." He could see the questions starting to form, and he had to admit, he kind of enjoyed provoking her.

"Who are Zoë and Veronica?" she demanded.

"My nieces." He smiled slyly. "Zoë is fourteen, and Veronica is eleven, but they're both going on thirty-five. They are holy terrors, and when we get back

to New York, you're going to be very sorry you have
to be nice to them.''

Annie chewed her lip, regarding him thoughtfully for
a moment. "They're the ones who wrote your essay,
aren't they? 'Awesome babe' and all that—it sounds
just like a couple of teenagers.''

"I suppose I might as well confess," he said
grudgingly.

"It all fits," she returned grandly. "And you went
along with all of this contest nonsense just to protect
them, didn't you? You're so gallant, it makes me sick
to my stomach.''

"That's my Annie. Always building me up with
compliments.''

"I try," she said sweetly, kissing his cheek.

Trevor pushed open the door to the familiar conference room, widening his eyes at the bounty of bright
pink balloons wafting around the ceiling. It was the
usual sort of Framboise occasion, with champagne and
raspberries everywhere, as well as a lot of that insufferable pink. Just inside the door, Kerenza was taking
bows, basking in the attention from the media, and
loudly proclaiming that she was very sure she'd be the
winner.

"Well, well, if it isn't our little lovebirds," she
sniffed, sweeping to the side so that not even the hem
of her garment could possibly be touching them. "I
would've thought you two had better things to do than
interfere with my press conference.''

"*Your* press conference?" Annie bristled, but Trevor
quickly pulled her past the princess and out of firing
range.

"Oh, my," he said, bending down to whisper in her
ear. "Get a load of Marie-Ange and Bertrand, over
there behind that big bunch of balloons. Talk about
lovebirds.''

"Marie-Ange looks years younger," Annie said defensively. "I think it's terrific. Now, be nice; they're headed this way."

"*Bonjour!*" the Frenchwoman said cheerfully. "So glad to see you, my friends. And, of course, you know Bertrand."

Her young assistant blushed deep red as he solemnly shook both their hands.

"By the way," Annie began. She had a funny little smile, and Trevor eyed her warily. "It may be a little strange, but I wanted to say thank you for not showing up at the penthouse. As you can probably tell, the ruse worked, and we're both very happy."

"Oh, it was nothing," Marie-Ange replied with a girlish giggle. "The one you should thank is Jamesina. She, after all, had the brilliant idea."

Annie pressed her lips into a frown. "Yes, I know," she muttered. "I just hate to encourage her."

Trevor knew she was still miffed at Jamie for tricking them, and she wasn't going to give in easily. He was ambivalent himself, although he did think Jamie deserved a good spanking for her interference. Nonetheless, she'd brought them together, and he couldn't fault that.

"You two look so wonderful together," the woman in question said gaily, hugging them both before they could dissuade her. "Oh, and Marie-Ange and Bertrand, too! Isn't this just too perfect?"

The little matchmaker beamed at them all, as if she were a proud mother sending her kiddies off to school. Yes, Trevor decided, she definitely ought to be spanked.

"Jamie," Annie said, with a chilly note in her voice. "Don't take this the wrong way, but I really think you should go back to writing books and leave real people alone."

"Pishposh. If I hadn't stepped in, you two would still be fighting over whether you should wear your seat belt on the airplane."

"I hate it when she's right," Annie grumbled.

Trevor just smiled his most mysterious smile, keeping Annie securely under his arm, where he could keep an eye on her.

"Listen, everyone!" Marie-Ange exclaimed, hastily beating a path back to the podium. "It is time to announce the winner of our 'Isn't It Romantic?' contest. If you would gather around, please, we can begin."

Annie crossed her arms over her chest. "Who needs an announcement? We all know Jamie won."

Her attitude was becoming annoying. He knew the contest was important to her, but he wasn't going to put up with all this surliness. He leaned over to whisper, "If you win, will you take me with you to all those exotic places?"

"I'm not going to win."

"If you do, I'm coming with you," he vowed.

"Done," she said saucily. "And if you win, I'm coming with you."

Trevor grinned. "Done."

Annie grinned right back. "Isn't it wonderful how good we are at negotiating?"

"It's all that practice." He couldn't resist a quick kiss. "For luck."

Marie-Ange cleared her throat loudly, as if to tell them to stop the shenanigans in the back of the room. "We've pored over the original essays," she informed them. "We have also carefully weighed the style and presentation of the events themselves."

"Style and presentation, huh?" Annie said darkly. "I told you Jamie was going to win."

"Be quiet."

Marie-Ange droned on, "Princess Kerenza's fantasy had a great deal of style, but very little substance. We're very sorry, Princess, but we decided, upon reflection, that yours was not the strongest entry."

"How dare you?" Kerenza bellowed. Quivering with indignation, she and her curves swept from the room.

"Style but no substance," Trevor remarked. "That's our princess."

"Mr. Case," the Framboise vice president interrupted. "Your entry was also stylish, and it sounded very romantic indeed from Miss Jonesborough's description. Unfortunately, the essay was not written as well as some of the others, and when choosing who would be our spokesperson, we felt we needed someone whose writing was more polished."

Annie choked back a giggle. "Those awesome babes will kill you every time," she whispered loudly. "Sorry, darling."

"And that leaves only Miss Jonesborough and Miss MacDougal," Marie-Ange continued. "Both essays were beautifully written, very evocative, and simply delightful, as are both of the authors." She bestowed a kind smile upon the two of them. "The judging committee felt that both of you showed imagination and a true understanding of the romantic spirit in the situations you chose."

"Get on with it," Annie muttered. "We all know they're going to pick Jamie."

He glared at her. "Shhhhh."

"It was a difficult decision, but we did have to make a choice in the end." Marie-Ange paused, and Trevor clenched his jaw. He'd told her it wasn't important, but deep down, he really wanted Annie to win. He stuffed a hand in his pocket and stared a hole in Marie-Ange, willing her to go on, and to say the right name. "We felt," she said briskly, "that Miss MacDougal's marvelous seventeenth-century fantasy—"

Beside him, Annie let out the breath she'd been holding. "I told you so."

"—was simply on too grand a scale. As our romance spokesperson, we felt we needed someone who understood romance on a more personal, more modern level."

Hope soared. Annie's fingers clenched his arm, and they both leaned forward to hear the rest.

"Therefore, it is with great pleasure that we introduce Miss Anna Jonesborough as the winner of our 'Isn't It Romantic?' contest, and the new Romance Ambassador for Framboise Champagne."

"I won! I won!" she shouted.

He couldn't hold back his triumphant smile as he peeled her fingers off his arm and prodded her forward. "They're waiting for you."

"I can't believe I won," she whispered.

But she took a deep breath and waltzed right up to the podium, like the polished, professional spokesperson she was going to be.

"Thank you very much. I'm really very honored and thrilled that you've chosen me." Her words might have been intended for the contest committee, but her eyes were practically glowing at Trevor. "I have honestly had the time of my life so far, and I'm looking forward to experimenting with a lot more of the romantic life."

Everybody applauded, as one of the reporters stepped forward. "And where will you be based?"

"Ah, New York, I think." She lifted an eyebrow at Trevor, and he nodded quickly. "New York," she said, with more conviction this time. "I'm planning to be married in the near future, and if we can work it out, I plan to bring my new husband along on my press appearances."

New husband? Trevor didn't know whether to laugh or cry. "It appears I'm getting married," he murmured, trying to weave through the crowd and get to Annie, as Framboise champagne was opened all around, with a great popping of corks and splashing of wine.

"Since when are we getting married?" he asked her, firmly taking her elbow and guiding her aside.

"We may already be married," she said delicately. "Remember the château and the priest?"

He didn't know whether to laugh or cry. He just

smiled. What else could he do? One way or the other he was going to be married to the woman he loved, they were going to travel to Rio and Rome together, and he couldn't imagine anything he'd like better.

Pitching his voice louder, he declared, "I would like to offer a toast."

"By all means," Marie-Ange responded.

"To Marie-Ange and Bertrand," he said. "Our gracious hosts, we wish you much happiness. To Kerenza . . ."

An audible groan filled the room.

"May she never darken our door again," he finished, amid much cheering. "To Jamie, whose fertile imagination promises much success in her chosen field."

He hesitated, long enough to find and hold her gaze. "And to Annie," he said with a sentimental smile. "The love of my life."

They all raised their glasses, floating in all that fine champagne, as Trevor pulled Annie into his arms and kissed her hungrily. Although he was very preoccupied with what he was doing, he couldn't miss the sound of Jamie's contented sigh.

Behind him, his favorite matchmaker said wistfully, "Isn't it romantic?"

SHARE THE FUN . . .
SHARE YOUR NEW-FOUND TREASURE!!

You don't want to let your new books out of your sight? That's okay. Your friends can get their own. Order below.

No. 165 PARIS WHEN IT SIZZLES by Julie Kistler
Annie was feisty! She was a challenge Trevor just couldn't pass up.

No. 108 IN YOUR DREAMS by Lynn Bulock
Meg's dreams become reality when Alex reappears in her peaceful life.

No. 109 HONOR'S PROMISE by Sharon Sala
Once Honor gave her word to Trace, there would be no turning back.

No. 110 BEGINNINGS by Laura Phillips
Abby had her future completely mapped out—until Matt showed up.

No. 111 CALIFORNIA MAN by Carole Dean
Quinn had the Midas touch in business but Emily was another story.

No. 112 MAD HATTER by Georgia Helm
Sara returns home and is about to make a deal with the man called Devil!

No. 113 I'LL BE HOME by Judy Christenberry
It's the holidays and Lisa and Ryan exchange the greatest gift of all.

No. 114 IMPOSSIBLE MATCH by Becky Barker
As Tyler falls in love with Chantel, it gets harder to keep his secret.

No. 115 IRON AND LACE by Nadine Miller
Shayna was not about to give an inch where Joshua was concerned!

No. 116 IVORY LIES by Carol Cail
April makes Semi a very unusual proposition and it backfires on them.

No. 117 HOT COPY by Rachel Vincer
Surely Kate was over her teenage crush on superstar Myles Hunter!

No. 118 HOME FIRES by Dixie DuBois
Leara ran from Garreth once, but he vowed she wouldn't this time.

No. 119 A FAMILY AFFAIR by Denise Richards
Eric had never met a woman like Marla . . . but he loves a good chase.

No. 120 HEART WAVES by Gloria Alvarez
Cass was intrigued by Peyton, one of the few who dared stand up to him.

No. 121 ONE TOUGH COOKIE by Carole Dean
Taylor Monroe was the type of man Willy had spent a lifetime avoiding.

No. 122 ANGEL IN DISGUISE by Ann Wiley
Sunny was surprised to encounter the man who still haunted her dreams.

No. 123 LIES AND SHADOWS by Pam Hart
Gabe certainly did not fit Victoria's image of the perfect nanny!

No. 124 NO COMPETITION by Marilyn Campbell
Case owed Joey Thornton a favor and now she came to collect his debt.

No. 125 COMMON GROUND by Jeane Gilbert-Lewis
Blaise was only one of her customers but Les just couldn't forget him.

No. 126 BITS AND PIECES by Merline Lovelace
Jake expected an engineering whiz . . . but he didn't expect Maura!

No. 127 FOREVER JOY by Lacey Dancer
Joy was a riddle and Slater was determined to unravel her mystery.

No. 128 LADY IN BLACK by Christina Dodd
The cool facade Margaret worked at so hard, melted under Reid's touch.

No. 129 TO LOVE A STRANGER by Blythe Bradley
Diana found her man but Trevor looked far from the villain she imagined.

No. 130 ALWAYS A LADY by Sharon Sala
Lily finds the peace and contentment she craves on Case's ranch.

Meteor Publishing Corporation
Dept. 893, P. O. Box 41820, Philadelphia, PA 19101-9828

Please send the books I've indicated below. Check or money order (U.S. Dollars only)—no cash, stamps or C.O.D.s (PA residents, add 6% sales tax). I am enclosing $2.95 plus 75¢ handling fee for *each* book ordered.

Total Amount Enclosed: $_____.

____ No. 165	____ No. 113	____ No. 119	____ No. 125
____ No. 108	____ No. 114	____ No. 120	____ No. 126
____ No. 109	____ No. 115	____ No. 121	____ No. 127
____ No. 110	____ No. 116	____ No. 122	____ No. 128
____ No. 111	____ No. 117	____ No. 123	____ No. 129
____ No. 112	____ No. 118	____ No. 124	____ No. 130

Please Print:
Name _____
Address _____ Apt. No. _____
City/State _____ Zip _____

Allow four to six weeks for delivery. Quantities limited.

Isn't It Romantic?

When Annie Porter received the letter from the Framboise Champagne Company, she was thrilled. She was a finalist! Her romantic fantasy was one of four chosen by the judges. If she made it through the next round, scheduled to take place in Paris, she would have the job as Framboise spokesperson, Romance Ambassador to the world. The news couldn't have come at a better time. Her job as a tabloid journalist was draining her skills, energy, and dignity. How many articles could one person write about Elvis, naughty princes, and aliens from the planet Zeegor?

Determined to beat out the competition, Annie met a formidable opponent in Trevor Case. A slick, high-profile trial attorney, "Casanova Case" was a winner in court and out. With a voice like velvet and steely gray eyes that could melt a woman's resolve, Case had a distinct advantage — a *male* advantage. Annie would have to fight to the end!

Trevor Case wasn't supposed to be involved in the contest. But just as he was about to withdraw his entry, he tangled with one of the feistiest women he'd met in years. Small, blond and dressed to kill, Annie presented a challenge — and that was one thing Trevor Case couldn't resist.

METEOR PUBLISHING CORPORATION

ISBN 1-56597-080-2

U.K.   £2.75